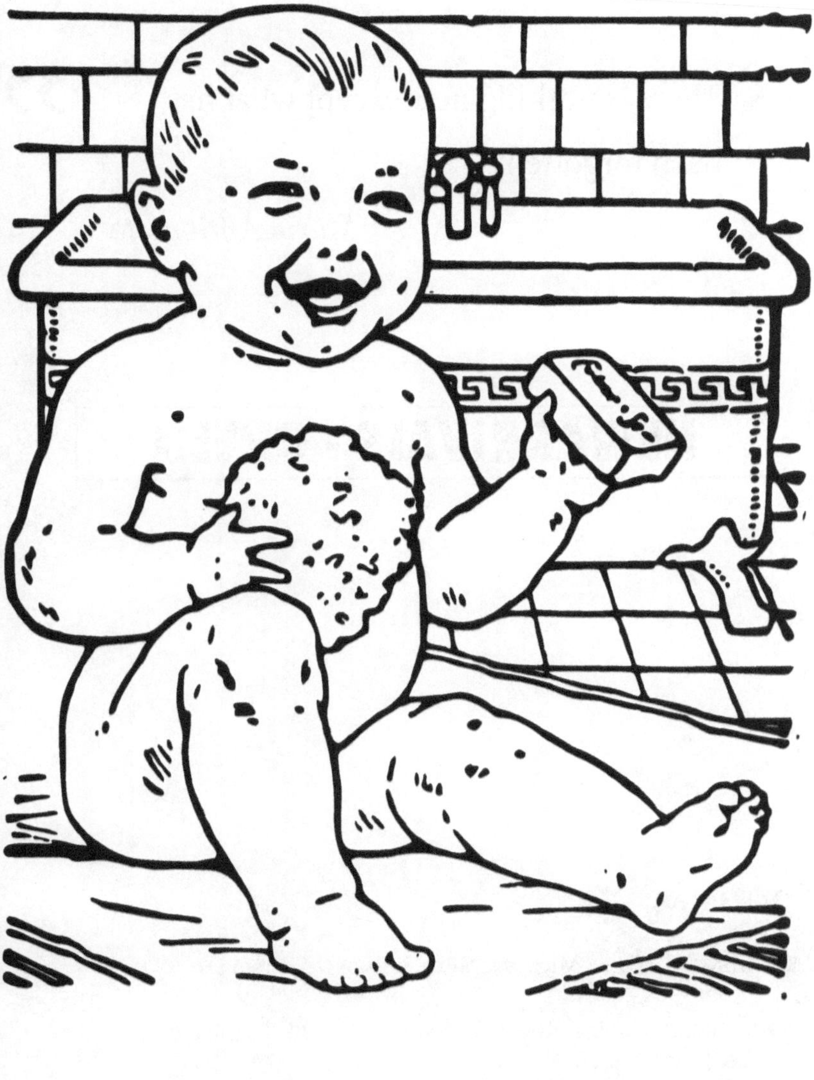

DEEP OVERSTOCK

#9: New Arrivals

July 2020

NEWARRIVALS - GREEN

EDITORIAL

MANAGING EDITORS: Mickey Collins & Robert Eversmann

PROSE: Mickey Collins, Robert Eversmann, Michael Santiago & Z.B. Wagman

POETRY: Ariel Kusby

TRANSLATION: Sue Su

COVER: Mickey Collins

CONTACT: editors@deepoverstock.com
deepoverstock.com

On the Shelves

[continued...]

Letter from the Editors

Dearest Readers,

Now that our ninth issue finished has been shelved, as it were, Deep Overstock is no longer a new arrival on the literary journal scene. Just for this issue alone we received submissions from booksellers and book lovers from all parts of the world: Australia, the Middle East, England, even Ohio! There were more short stories, poems, and pieces of flash fiction than we had room for. In this time of Covid-19 and quarantine it is a beautiful sight to see writers and artists are not giving up.

In this "themeless" issue, our contributors have brought some brand new writing and art that cover all sorts of topics. We hope that you enjoy the pieces collected here and that they can bring you some much needed--at least in our case--distraction.

And don't think that just because we did an issue that was open themed we have run out of ideas. Pish posh! The next theme for Deep Overstock will be… The Origin of Life! Submit your pieces by September 1st, 2020!

Deep Overstock Editors

Bingo Bitch
by Dianah Hughley

Sometimes people become friends simply by chance. She was in her 60s and we were 10 or 11 when we first met her. Even though she wasn't related to us, we called her Nanny; just like everyone else did. By the time we met her, Nanny's life was almost over. Fifteen or so years is not long enough to spend with a friend, but that was all we got.

Through the years, we spent many days at her house; we in our cool new school clothes, she slouched on her couch, in her "flouncer" and slippers. We would watch tv, smoke, eat, tell her about our crushes, laugh at her stories; always deep in conversation. Late into the night, we would climb the staircase and fall asleep in her pink ruffled bedrooms, wake very late the next day and repeat the cycle. She called us her stooges.

As a young woman, she was stunned when she sent her husband out one evening to buy chicken for dinner, but instead, he vanished. Her "one true love" just disappeared into the night; never to return, never to come home. He left her alone and devastated with three young daughters in tow. After that, much of her life was a struggle, yet she raised her three daughters and a granddaughter with something like sheer determination.

She was a tidy housekeeper. She was a good cook. She loved her weekly trips to Kmart. She only shaved her legs for the doctor -- hilarious to us, all those years ago. She would only take her pills with buttermilk; to which we would pantomime vomiting. Her sense of humor was scathing and we loved it. Her favorite thing was bingo; once a week -- never, ever missing it. B-11 was always calling her name.

Nanny's philosophy was "life is a party" -- a big bingo game. Have fun while you're here and get out when you're done. Follow the rules. Don't get too greedy. Play your favorites. Sometimes they never call your number. Sometimes you're "on" all night. Mostly you lose, but sometimes you win. It's still fun to play either way. Go home when you're out of money. You can play again next week.

Her second husband wasn't the best man, but he was bearable. She waited on him while swallowing her pride; truly grateful for the security he provided. They fought angrily as they grew older together, but she somehow kept her sense of humor. Her husband regularly called her a "feisty old bitch." During one heated argument he flung the nickname "Bingo Bitch" at her. It stuck. She laughed out loud at that one.

Even though Nanny was old fashioned and had her own set of morals, she was not naive to the sometimes tragic decisions of teenagers. She had "street smarts" and common sense. She paid for her granddaughter's abortion. She knew we were wasting our lives with sex, alcohol, shoplifting, ditching school, and drugs. She disapproved; sometimes quietly and sometimes very vocally. But we were her stooges and she loved us anyway.

When her second husband died, she moved away, and we didn't see her much after that. We would sometimes drive up to her new duplex to visit. She sat hunched over on her old couch like always, but her choice of clothing was not her flouncer: she had dressed for our visits. I guess by then she considered us company.

Eventually pneumonia left her in the hospital, and it played havoc with her. We were afraid for her, and for us. She had IVs and monitors attached to her, and tubes down her nose and throat. Those tubes left her without a voice, which was a rare and painful situation for Nanny. She relied mostly on hand signals, and occasionally wrote things down on paper. When she choked from the fluid in her lungs, she did so without making a sound: her body wracked, but silent. We stood by helpless as the nurses bent over her. She kept making a curious pinching motion with her fingers. This meant she wanted her lungs suctioned out, because she couldn't breathe; that frantic, futile pinching; over and over she pinched and pinched, helpless and frightened. The nurses blocked our view of her face, but we could clearly see those frenzied, trembling fingers pinching in vain.

When they told us her body was shutting down and it
wouldn't be long, we didn't realize they meant within the week.
When we saw her lying in her bronze casket with eyes closed,
we remembered her sitting on her couch, in her flouncer, with
eyes open. She looked the same.

What must it feel like when you can't take a breath?

A Quiet Place in the Rain
by Nicholas Yandell

A quiet place in the rain,

To be alone,

With cold,
Damp,
Companions,
Holding exposed,

The virtues of isolation.

Numbness dissipates,
Distraction,
Escape,
Lulled away…

A soft static wash,

In the soundscape.

Chill flows,
Shivers of urgency,
Dislodging buried slivers,
Coaxing them to the surface,
Embracing *Affliction*,
And the wisdom of *Weariness*,
Cast stubborn *Comfort* aside,
At the onset of the journey.

Take the hand of *Lonesome's* soldier,
A courier to seek out,
Consolation's elusive route,
Through clouded corners of the map.

Scale the peaks of *Trepidation*,
Cross raging rivers of *Doubt*,

Carry on through the draught,
In the sands of *Abandonment*…

                                  Descend,
The deepest frozen caverns,
Lay before *Desperation's* icy claws.
Gritting teeth,
      Waking skin,
            Bracing to begin,

            The quenching,
                  Cleansing,
                        Trial.

            The body releases,
            Surfacing desires,
      Shockwave comprehension,
            Baptizing,
            Naked,
            Immersion,
            Downpouring,
Storm's fluid gospel.

            Incite,
                  Anaesthetized urges,
                  Allowing Darkness's glue,
                        To mend the invisible cracks,
                              Lost to light-addled eyes,
                              And dayglow existence.

Rise up,
      Pulsing,
            Emerging,
                  From a pilgrimage,
                  Offering exchange:

            Suffering for relief;

            Dissolution for restoration;

            Helplessness,
                  Against the elements,
                        For that sturdy,

Slowly-growing,
Seed of *Freedom*,

Only the shadow-drenched soul,

Will ever know.

A Few Days After Becoming a Vampire

by Kummam Al-Maadeed

1:49 a.m.

We sat silently on his balcony. Two fresh victims lay on the floor between our chairs.

He lit a cigar and offered it to me. I took it.

I never liked these things, but after the transformation I longed for the feeling of air breezing inside of me.

A feeling I never thought I would miss.

I inhaled deeply and slowly exhaled a cloud of smoke.

And we sat there staring at the sky glowing with city lights.

I've been living in his penthouse since the day he took me from the parking lot.

"Why me?" I asked him that day. "Why did you change me?"

"It was your cat. She suggested you," he replied as he showed me the place.

I couldn't decide whether I hated or loved her for that.

I mean I was a vampire. I was a supernatural. I've always dreamed it.

But I never realized how annoying the logistics were.

He, Ahmad, the original vampire, had to modify my family's memories so they'd think I was studying abroad.

I had to email a resignation letter to Jana and Ahmad had

to sneak into her apartment, which he said was horribly messy, and compel her to accept my resignation without a question.

There were also the logistics of kidnapping and eating people. That was a headache.

But he was good at it. He had been doing it for more than a decade.

I stared at him. His sharp chiseled face. If this was a teen show, he would be the favorite mysterious vampire ready to be redeemed once he found his one true love.

This wasn't a show. I wasn't his true love and he wasn't my favorite.

"Why do you even wear the suit?" I blurted. I was holding the question inside of me for days.

He raised an eyebrow and glanced down at his attire.

"It's what vampires wear." He simply said it.

"In the movies?"

"Yes." He smiled, his cigar stuck between his teeth.

Yup, he was just another pertinacious douche.

I sighed and stood up. I moved closer to the railing.

"So, you only made me a vampire to be your companion?" I asked, leaning forward.

"Yes." He puffed a cloud of smoke. "I've been like this for a very long time and I felt lonely."

I hummed, scanning the city, the hundreds of thousand of hearts beating together in perfect harmony.

It was my favorite song.

"What if I didn't want to just be that," I said, slow and serious.

He got up and stood beside me, his back on the railing and his head leaning closer to mine.

"You don't want this life? We're free to just be."

"No. I don't want to just be. I want more," I whispered, a plan forming in my head.

"And that is?" he chuckled in a douchey annoying way.

"I …" I stood up and licked my fangs. "I'm going to build me a kingdom."

16 *Untitled - Jeremy Szuder*

Altamaha

by Matthew Hunt

It is no small thing to be forgotten.
After centuries of birth, and endless ghosts,
To find oneself without a gathering,
A narrative of beginning and purpose,
Stumps that rise from depthless silt,
Crawling, like the first creatures, onto the land,
We bred what impulses for air were held on our lips,
Breath, and endless heartbeats, arose from the push
Of oar into ripple, of foot onto sand, of the groaning
Of weight against the slow and endless current,
Draining blackness and heat from the piedmont,
Thick and oppressive as history, or the air that sits
Unmoving, like August, like the Precambrian,
Buried in alluvial time, its violence unseen,
Dropping in eddies barely rounded,
To the deep and deeper dream that time
May be measured and felt.

Great cities might have risen in lands both far and old,
To drain and to feed the estuaries and the tides
Or demand their return to the quaysides,
Laden with stocks and the bangles of trade
The river is the bridge as well as the chasm, and flow little
matters
To the pulse of export and desire.

But all is noiseless, save for the water's break
To capture the hatch of midge, rising in late morning,
Or the chorus of cicadas, electric in the evening hum.
None have found their way,
Though all around the freeways beat
With that same steady throb
This land is dark and unknowable,
Even to those few who trespass here.

Forget, and forget
That we ever trod the wilds, that we ever tamed their secrets,

Exposed them as fraudulent superstition,
Here there is no dream of light,
No shafts that break the low moors or thickets,
Worm into the astringent drifts of the bitter waters,
Drawing the skin around the bones like a desert
The broad and dimming floods that cover all with life,
Yet bury like the endless sands,
The night is not endless, but it is unyielding,

Forget and forget these unclaimed wilds,
And that there are wilds still.

where the heat goes when it rises

by ellie sharp

we build home out of half a whatever.
a deck of cards smeared across the asphalt
our hands slapping wildly like flying fish.
a watery tongue spills over the rock ledge
and licks at the salt of our spilled trail mix.

i'd write to the water but i'd be wrong.
we don't come for the tides or shore but the scorching
concrete. the lake is six miles from the sun and wants
to become an ocean. it's been rising since graduation
so we don't swim anymore

just stand on the ledge and pretend to jump, hands held and sweaty.
train delays everywhere in a smouldering city so we'll stay here
waiting for everyone we know to walk by.

the sun comes up for air between scaffolds of clouds.
we scoot back when the lake rises. no worries. it's not the ash's fault,
the water returns here same as us.

when you get here, we'll go somewhere else to sit.
night comes to the shore first so we walk too far for stars
to follow and end up dangled across dawn's gazebo.
whoever isn't here will be there,
all of us swimming in time.

20 *Bookstore Window, rue de Lille, Paris 7° - Roger Camp*

Death and Life
by Erin Kratina Karbuczky

The day she killed herself should have been the best day of her life so far. It was Monday afternoon, and on Monday evening, she was set to have the soft launch of her very first book kickoff at the local bookstore. Pre-orders had been strong, and her publisher had pushed for this debut, hard. She never felt more supported and never felt more alone.

In the morning, her husband ran for bagels and coffee and told her she was beautiful. After breakfast, he took their daughter to the park so she could get ready alone and have the space to freak out. When his car left the driveway she took the razor to her wrists in the shower. This was not the first time she cut herself, but it would be the last. Six cut-free years down the drain.

When Jake and Maggie (not Margaret) came home, Maggie went straight to the couch to watch her favorite cartoon and down goldfish crackers, disregarding the wash your hands when you come in the house rule. And for good reason - had she walked into her parents' bathroom to wash her hands, she would have found her mother slumped over the edge of the tub, eyes lifeless and body limp.

Instead, it was Jake who found her and held her body and reached for his cell to call the police.

No one notified the bookstore.

At about 7:30 pm, a half hour after the event was supposed to start, the author had not shown up, nor had she called to alert anyone to a late arrival. The owner and sole employee, Veronica, took the microphone and said, "I believe we've been stood up. I'm sorry for any inconvenience. I will happily give refunds to anyone who is unsatisfied…" and she wondered how she would get the publisher to take the unsold and returned books back. She also ruminated on the fact that she had brought out the good wine and cheese for this event, because the book had stirred her emotions and brought back her own creative side again.

"I am so disappointed," said Ruth, a regular at the store. She was in her seventies, and most of her free time was spent wandering the stacks, looking for the cheapest copy of Oprah's latest book club pick. "I was looking forward to this event. My daughter told me to stay home tonight because I have a cold, but I couldn't wait to meet the author. Is there going to be a discount or coupon for those of us who made the trip? And do you have a copy of *All the Light We Cannot See*?" She took a crinkled, hardened tissue out of her pocket and sniffled into it.

Veronica sighed. She stopped typing her email to her representative at Penguin and walked Ruth to fiction. "It's by Doerr," Veronica said. How many times had she told Ruth that the books were alphabetical by author?

A few days later the store phone rang about an hour after close. Veronica was staying late to straighten up and work on the budget.

"Sylvia's Bookshop," she said, wrinkling her nose at the sight of Ruth's tissue, now on the store carpet.

"Hello, I'm looking for a Ms. Veronica Birch?" the caller sounded smooth as whiskey and cologne, and also like he was holding back tears.

"This is she," she said.

"I apologize for the late notice, but… you had an event on Monday, right? And no author came?"

"That's right…"

"She… she's my wife. She killed herself Monday. I'm sorry I didn't call sooner. I couldn't… I wasn't able to talk."

Veronica had no idea what to say, so she said what she always said when someone slighted her, no matter their reason. "Okay."

"Is there… anything I can do? Can I buy the books you didn't sell? I'm sure you had some angry customers."

"As a matter of fact," Veronica said. "I can't return them. So I would love for you to take them off my hands." As an afterthought, she said "Sorry about your wife."

Jake felt bad, and then he laughed despite himself. Why did he feel bad for Veronica? Yes, she suffered a bit financially, but his wife was DEAD for fuck's sake.

Jake hung up after making an appointment to pick up the books. He wondered what exactly he would do with fifty copies of his wife's book? The only other copy in his house was an advanced reader. It had come in late July when the family was on vacation, and the sun had melted the packaging a bit. Alicia's face had blurred on the back of the book, the skin-toned ink leaking down from her author photo into the red background. He checked on Maggie, asleep in her room, the night-light making star and moon shapes on her face, which was morphing into his wife's face by the minute. He closed her door and went into his room and took his wife's laptop off of her desk. She gave him the password just recently when she asked him to retrieve a document from the computer.

When he logged in, the most recent tab on her Chrome was a document simply entitled "Journal."

Alicia kept journals starting when she was about fourteen, and ending only when she died. There was even an entry from that fateful Monday morning.

"I feel like I should be on top of the world right now, but inside I want to die."

Was she ever happy? He wondered. He had known her for so long, but it was damn near impossible to read her. Now was his chance. He went into the closet and took out the giant rubbermaid tote and took her journals out in piles. A few years ago she had went through them and labeled them in order, 1 to 30, with approximate dates. He set aside her journals from ages fourteen to eighteen, but at nineteen things got interesting.

That's when she began to write fiction.

Before long, he had discovered three novels, enough poetry for two collections, a trove of song lyrics, fifteen short stories, and twenty fragments of yet-to-be started projects. He also discovered that she had an affair a few years ago, around the time they got pregnant with Maggie. He was supposed to be making funeral arrangements right now. He felt like he was supposed to idolize his wife now that she was gone, but he was instead reveling in how gloriously human she was. If she were alive, he would have been angry at the discovery of betrayal. But now, this was like smelling her perfume on a sweatshirt. It was like entering her for the first time. It was sobbing into her neck, or holding her hair back when she threw up during her pregnancy.

There was no question about Maggie. She had his eyes and his sense of humor. He had raised her since she was born, and he planned to continue to do so. There was no need to question paternity. But he did wonder about publishing Alicia's work.

Echoing his thoughts, her agent said, "It would be a shame to not shop around those previously rejected manuscripts. The market changes all the time. What was rejected before, might be rejoiced now." And the agent went to work, shopping around the manuscripts in his filing cabinet and email, asking publishers to JUMP on this HOT, POSTHUMOUS WORK. JUVENALIA. MARGINALIA. JOURNALS. PURCHASE GENIUS LITERATURE BEYOND YOUR WILDEST DREAMS.

And the publishers leapt like dogs in heat and bid and bid higher and higher.

Jake did not know he was sitting on a million dollar's worth of writing. If he had, he would have shut this thing down immediately. No one could put a price on his wife, even if she was fading from the forefront of his mind, rapidly.

A few weeks after her death, he found himself at Veronica's apartment with a bottle of wine and a brick of local cheese, and some conversation crackers.

Veronica let out a horsey laugh when she opened the door. It was the exact type of wine and cheese she wasted on the book launch that never was.

"On a more serious note," she said, raspy. "I saw on Pub Weekly that you're getting upwards of a million dollars if you sell your wife's life's work! That's a silver lining for sure." As soon as she said it she felt like an idiot. Silver lining? He just lost his wife.

"I'm sorry," she said. "I shouldn't have said that."

"It's okay," he said, and tucked his hair behind his ear, wanting to tuck her hair behind her ear. He felt himself wanting her, despite (or because of?) his grief, despite his perpetually watery eyes. Despite only having booked the sitter for two hours. He was only supposed to pick up the books. What was he doing here at her apartment, upstairs from the bookshop?

"How much did the books cost?"

She gives him a number, feeling awkward now. She was charging a widower for his dead wife's books because she couldn't sell them, even though by now everyone wanted to buy the books, and she would have to order more from the publisher anyway.

"Do you actually… things have changed since we last spoke. I can sell the books now… you know, it's like Kurt Cobain…" she wasn't making any sense. Jake wasn't sure how to respond verbally. So instead he kissed her, and then felt like an idiot. But she responded in kind. And that's how he ended up in Veronica's bed, mere weeks after his beloved slit her wrists, taking her last jagged breaths as she died, thinking god knows what.

When he got home and paid the sitter, he decided it just wasn't right to sell his wife's work. If she didn't get to enjoy the fruits of her labor, he didn't either. The next morning he asked the agent to stop shopping Alicia's work, and to destroy it. A media frenzy would have followed, but by then the story had died down, so to speak. There were so many new news stories each day, his own was buried.

Two months after that fateful Monday, he took Maggie into the yard, where he had lit a bonfire containing his wife's journals and works. The only evidence of her work existed on her laptop, which he had scanned every page onto before collecting it for the fire. He made hot cocoa "the special way, Mom's way," three mugs of it. He held his daughter tight and they reminisced, both of them laughing and crying, sometimes at the same time. Maggie said her heart felt like it was being tugged by her mother in heaven, and Jake laughed, because he and Alicia didn't talk about religion with Maggie, and certainly not the concept of heaven and hell, which neither of them believed in. But now, he wondered if heaven was real, and if Alicia really could see her husband and daughter from her perch among the stars. Joy pulled at his own cardiac muscle when he looked behind him. Veronica came through the back door with wine and cheese, and introduced herself to young Maggie, who had just moments before wished on a shooting star for a new mother.

Felita and the Green Bean

by Laura Scott

It was summer and the heater was on. Bob couldn't turn it off. The 1947 Pontiac he was driving chugged along on flat open road. The car had been restored from brown, back to its original colors, teal and seafoam. Before the restoration, we had known these colors were the car's birthright. We had seen them, still hiding, on the insides of the shit-brown doors. We had christened the car the Green Bean, and this was its maiden voyage in its new green coat, its heater broken and decidedly on. From my vantage point in the car behind him, I could see Bob's hand going up to wipe the sweat off his forehead with a white handkerchief, or drinking water from a flask my mother had filled that morning. It was like this for miles, wiping and watering. The road stretched itself out lazily before us, knowing it had nowhere to go but straight on. The clouds rolled by on the Green Bean's rounded tail fins and the whole cumulus-filled sky was reflected in seafoam. This was Montana, and we were chugging west.

At school in Wisconsin, we had studied about the Lakota Sioux Indians of South Dakota. They believed that west was the direction of death because west is the direction the sun sets in. In the car, looking out the window, I thought about that. It meant that we were traveling in the direction of death. Maybe not death for us, but death for our old new life, back in Wisconsin. Now we were travelling to our new old life, back to the place we had originally moved from: the west coast. For my parents, traveling west meant traveling in the direction of natural progression, of promotion. For me, traveling back meant moving in the direction of ambivalence. I was going back to where I had come from, but I was leaving something behind.

"Can I sit up with Bob?"

My mother looked at me peripherally, concentrating on the road in front of her, straight or not. "Why?"

"I want to see how hot it is."

She had no response but to follow Bob to the next rest area and pull off. We stopped frequently to make sure the Green Bean's radiator was holding out. I climbed up into the old car, leaving my mother and spaniel behind in the other car's air conditioning. It was hot, and I contemplated getting out again, 15-year-old curiosity satisfied. But it was a brief moment, and I stubbornly stuck to my plan. Only the exterior of the car had been restored, leaving the interior and those in it to fend for themselves forty years later. The heater was under the old brown-upholstered seat, and inside, the Green Bean was baking. It was too hot to talk, almost too hot to breathe, an action which, in itself, produced an unpleasant effect. The musty smell of ancient fabric, the roasting heater, and the odd half-smoked cigar in the ashtray produced a stale smell that stuck to the inside of my nose for hours afterward. There wasn't much point in opening the windows very wide, the temperatures inside and out were so evenly matched, but we left them down all the way to hear the sound of the air moving by, the tires on the road. But this too was pointless. Even more unavoidable than the heat was the music my step-father was playing. Marty Robbins. Through the plinks and twangs of a hopelessly unhappy guitar, I learned about the west Texas town of El Paso and a woman named Felita. She had loved him but left him. Rode off on his horse.

We continued traveling west, the Rockies behind us. Looking at the map of the western United States, I calculated that we would arrive in California in three days' time. Although it was the place we had come from, it wasn't our final destination. It was a kind of way station to visit our family and rest before making the final leg of the journey to Oregon and the new home that waited for us there. I had to set aside my reservations about the coming weeks and stare out the window, inhaling the heat. Being the new person was not new to me, and the only thing for it was to take a deep breath and smile and say hello, no matter what that felt like on the inside. And there was something else. I was leaving behind people. Friends. I had known them for two years, but when you're in middle school and high school, that's a long time. And one person in particular.

Now, in the car, the old music and stale heat made me drowsy. I thought again of Felita. We had a lot in common, she and I. I had loved somebody. Loved him and left him, too, although not in the way that Felita had loved or left Marty Robbins. I had loved him in the notes-in-school-locker, late-for-dinner, warm-mouthed, leaves-tangled-in-hair way that 15 year olds do. I had left him in the way that my parent's job decided I should leave. Pulling away from our house, it's bright red "sold" sign painfully obvious, my mother had looked out the rearview mirror and cried along with me at the sight of the boy waving goodbye. I think maybe she had known that backward wave, and I think she had understood.

Does it truly matter? Essentially, it does not, and if you asked me now, these many years later, I have memories of that time that are mostly visuals of the epic scenery between here and there: The soft-shoeing of glaciers through Yosemite and their carvings on the rocks; the wild hillside flowers as we climbed Colorado; the craggy outcroppings at the top of Devil's Monument in Wyoming where we all secretly thought of alien abductions, and the tiny remote towns, like Blue Earth, Minnesota, and its tiny diner with red-checked table cloths where everyone knows your name, and if they don't, they all stop to check you out. It does not matter in any other way except this: transition builds us. I move forward best by saying goodbye well, by remembering kindly, by transitioning to what I can learn next. I know this now. I think I knew it then too. The cheeks were tear-stained, of course, but tanned and uplifted, still. Riding along in that ridiculously hot car, I looked as far as I could see ahead. I imagined myself, Felita, with a red rose behind my ear, riding side-saddle, off into the sunset and into the west, defiant in the face of the direction of death.

The Teenage Magus

By Patrick Wray

ves stare blank at a drab fantasia
dust particles that move before his
es. The fusion of boy and machine
ay soon be completed even though it
rves no known purpose.'
is is brill! It must be part of Neil's
vel!
His vision turned all red. The world
looked like a photo developing room.
Their screams and cries merged to
resemble a petulant laugh.
My brother is clearly some sort of
genius but I've been so caught up
in myself , I guess I just never
realised.
Rory can you come and meet me? It's about
my brother. I think he may be some sort of
literary genius. His stuff is kind of Rimbaud
meets Ballard with a bit of Parsons.
The escalator seemed to
dissappear into space
looming over an endless
motorcade that snaked
across the frozen land.
How are
you son?
Well, I can't say fairer than
that can I?
Well Tracy, I suppose I have got nothing
to lose by taking a look, but I can't
make any promises.
Surviving the misery while still
contemplating the mystery of
everyday existence....
On the downside, my creative
writing is stuck in a void.
Don't be so hard on yourself bro. I think you
might just be one of the great literary minds
of the century. Faulks, Rushdie, Self. They
are all just a bunch of middlebrow crapola
chancers compared to you if you ask me.
ter on...
Who the hell are you and what do
you want?
Get the hell away from me! If you think I'd
patronise your rotten little rag with my
writing you must be mad! I'm a philosopher
and a writer of substance and depth, not
some little desperado punk looking for a
pen pal. Now sod off!!!
My name is Rory Molloy. I'm a friend
of your sisters. I'm the literary
editor of 'The Twonky' ; the school
magazine. We are always on the
lookout for new writers and I
wondered if you might be interested
in contributing some of your work?
Well, we all have to start
somewhere Neil. I just thought
that with Rory's help you might...

You know what Neil Sleet? I don't think you have the right attitude to be a writer in the modern world. You need to be prepared to market yourself. Being a literary outlaw is all well and good but it's not good PR when you are just starting out you know?
If I want to ruin my career before it's even begun, that's up to me, now stay out of it!
In boredoms ninth room he spied an old friend named dissapointment.
Oh disappointment I anoint thee, oh disappointment I appoint thee for one day thee shall be my closest friend.
The trouble is Rory; he doesn't really know what he wants. He is so consumed by his creative energies that he lashes out at anything that he percieves as a threat to his integrity .
Is that another extract from 'Wires' or what?
I think I know someone who might be able to help him.
Hey, I was chatting to that nice lad Rory Molloy from The Twonky and it seems all might not be lost.
He saw them all for what they were now. Fixed expressions trapped inside a million pieces of broken glass that lay scattered across the ocean floor.
Er, did you hear what I just said?
All sound was an electronic high pitch, a blizzard of TV fuzz. A primeval hum that came from some wretched factory that lay deep within the belly of the earth, where the land was run by some ancient machine older than the world itself.

So I'm guessing you'd be up for talking to him again then?
He turned away from it's gaze but everywhere he looked was consumed by it still. He could not move, paralysed, his eyes transfixed by a cracked mirror vision of humanity caving in on itself.
Well he hasn't said as much but I get from his general tone that he wants you to give him another chance.
Is there any sort of advance offered if his work is accepted for publication? I'm pretty confident that it will be.
I'm dressing in all black from now on. It's gonna go well with my whole tortured writer shtick.
That's the spirit!
Sad eyes observe a landscape of old faces and flaccid cocks. Emptiness and emptiness of cardboard boxes.
That's a bit crude isn't it?
That's not crude, that's poetry that is sis! Hey, check out this free ad. Some bloke is getting rid of a load of old TV sets! They could come in handy for my auto-destructive art project.
Never mind that. Here comes Rory with that friend of his he wanted you to meet.
Alright Neil.
Hi, I'm Janet. I'm the sub-editor of The Twonky. Rory asked me if I would help you with editing some of your writing for publication.
Well, I don't think my work needs much editing to be honest but...
Well even the best writers can benefit from a good editor sometimes Neil.
Well it looks like our plan worked. I knew that Janet would be able to sweet talk him around.
Are we still good for a sixty forty split on any future publishing royalties?
THE END

We Shared a Bed of Broken Glass

by J. Ian Bush

I used to have a friend who was full of busted light bulbs
some of them I assume were hereditary (his parents were both
black holes) but others he collected himself he treated his
anatomy like a trash bag shoveled in as much dead light as it
could hold once I saw him unhinge his jaw swallow the remains
of 100 wits without flinching eventually the pressure of swal-
lowing made the glass snap turned his lungs into a series of stab
wounds lined the insides with grains of sand his skin spouted a
garden of shards made everything he touched bleed

King Sneferu's Ring

by Maev Barba

On a fishing expedition, Sneferu gave a maiden a golden ring.

She slid the ring onto her finger, then, thinking better of it, slid it off and dropped it in the Nile.

Stop the boat, she said. And retrieve my ring.

This is Pharaoh Sneferu, the men said.

He built the Bent Pyramid, they said.

And then the Red Pyramid, they said.

And now he has given you his favorite ring.

Clouds obscured the light and the maiden turned away.

I know, she said, that you have a million of those rings.

Sneferu was not a callous man, nor did he disbelieve in magic.

You and you, he said. He ordered two men holding staffs and wearing beards.

These, perhaps the same who later challenged Moses, dipped their staffs into the water.

The Nile parted end to end. The boat teetered on the edge of water.

Sneferu reached between the Nile and retrieved the ring from where it nested in the rocks.

Dry it, said the maiden. Before you slide it on my finger.

Driving to Thom Young's House

by Scott Laudati

I heard there were no gun laws in Texas

so I rented a Taurus and drove

to Thom Young's house,

running over prairie dogs and singing the new

Blake Shelton Christmas song.

And when I got there

I bought a rifle and some nightcrawlers

and we fished in a puddle behind the Allsup's.

But the fish didn't want any worms

and on the drive back

Thom said Led Zeppelin wouldn't make it today.

And I remembered the music

and how it had lived in me once

and in my dreams

I can still hear my mother sing it like

she's hanging over my crib.

And sometimes the college radio

comes in clear from Amarillo

and Thom finds an old box of tobacco

and we smoke like kings without thrones,

flicking ash at the coyotes circling the porch.

Once upon a time betting on

whether it would be them

or us

but we don't play that game as much anymore.

And on cold Sundays after Christmas

we leave burritos outside for the dogs.

The Man Called Sue
by Lily Bradfield

He walked up to the mic stand slowly, deliberately—he didn't look like someone who did karaoke, and yet here he was. He didn't belong in the beer-drenched hall, enclosed in an expensive navy blue suit, tie knotted just so under his Adam's apple. But despite his buttoned-upness, his hair was overgrown and floppy—that of a young boy who refused to sit still in the barbershop chair. He had come straight from work, you could tell, his briefcase abandoned at the side of the stage and exhaustion set underneath his eyes.

And so he climbed up there, pressed suit and wild hair, and picked his song. It took a long time, and a charged silence filled the crowded room, a specific kind of silence that comes only with the absence of music in a karaoke bar. One where you can hear clearly the shifting of young people in their seats, their attention turning away from the stage and toward their phones.

And then his song started. Twangy, and slightly old-fashioned. Those who frequented this bar, on Avenue A in the Lower East Side of Manhattan, were used to synthesized Top 40 hits. But this was not that. A guitar, only, and the sound of a live audience. He picked it because it was the song that his dad had played for him, on long rides in the car of his youth, the car (and the father) he left behind when he moved away for college in the city. The audience didn't know this, of course, he had no one in the crowd to know this. But you could see it, a little, in the way he seemed to loosen at the sound of the strings.

The man started tapping his shiny, wing-tipped Oxford to the beat. A little off-tempo. Bobbing his head disjointedly, just enough so that his hair flopped, almost comically, this way and that. You could picture him, this grown man, as a child in the passenger side of his father's car, even if you didn't know him. Just from the nodding of his head. The colored lights glinted off the disco ball and drifted across his lapel.

It was a Johnny Cash song. Almost all spoken dialogue.
A little silly in its blatant Americana—all fist fights and lost
fathers and booze. But the man had such an earnest look on his
face that it made the song instantly, easily loved. And he did the
voice, too, with a barstool-cowboy gruffness. Learned from his
father, and cherished. A sheepish bravado.

He slowly started to shed—first the jacket, thrown onto
the sticky bar floor, and then the tie was loosened and the top
buttons undone and the shirtsleeves rolled up to his elbows. He
came out of himself until his hair matched his clothes, like an
overgrown altar boy eager to ditch church and get back to the
neighborhood baseball game.

And then he was dancing. Holding the mic stand, dipping
it like it was his very own dance partner. His long-stiff limbs—
you could tell he hadn't moved like this in a while—suddenly,
awkwardly, beautifully, free.

By the end he was panting, rosy-cheeked. The song ended,
and he stood there, so different from when he first stepped onto
the stage. The room was quiet for a moment. He looked at his
shoes, bashful, then moved from the spotlight. And then every-
one, slowly, everyone clapped. And he smiled, quietly proud.
And satisfied, so satisfied.

Place

by Jesse Sensibar

Hunkering down on a steel gray October day on a mural of B.B. King that Bobby Sutton painted at the end of Promontory Point. Having a smoke and looking all the way to where the water and the sky meet. The rap of strait pipes echoing off the worn-out brick buildings on Erving Park at 5:30 A.M. Setting in scrub oak on the edge of an abandoned back forty on a Sunday in Michigan in November with your Daddy's old side by side 16 gauge in your hands watching a big buck move out of range.

Standing on a gently swaying dock in Sharp Rock inlet watching the last float plane get airborne. Lying on the hood of your Chevy pick-up with your back against the windshield on top of that hill in the middle of Hart Prairie. Drinking cheap beer and watching the storm roll in from all directions. Drinking coffee in the pre-dawn darkness in the kitchen of an old farm house in the middle of nowhere listening to your truck warm up. Never having to say "look" or "I know" or "I'm sorry." Never having to say anything.

Man Eater

by Melissa Kerman

Umberto's cooks the juiciest veal cutlet in the entire city. You know this because you've eaten veal cutlet at every Italian restaurant in the entire city. You've given second chances; with the sand-haired boy two weeks ago you revisited Butera's and then Pomodorino with the freckled boy last week, but at both places the dish still tasted like copper. As you sipped your third glass of Merlot and feasted on cold garlic bread, you realized *this* is why you stick with what you know won't disappoint.

At 7:50 you peer over your steering wheel as your date shuffles toward the restaurant. He had offered to pick you up, but you told him you live far so you'd meet him instead. It's safer this way. Your date fiddles with his bomber jacket collar. His posture rivals the Hunchback and although you're parked yards away, you can tell he's not six feet tall like his profile claims. Maybe five ten, at most. Strike one.

What else is he lying about?

You unlock your phone, pausing to recall which dating app you two matched on. Ah, yes. Now you remember. You open his profile. You conduct your research in the days prior, but it's useful to brush up that evening. *Looking for a smart girl to make dumb decisions with.* Not your first encounter with that tagline, but you prefer a cliched bio over an exhaustive info dump and the photos are what determine your swipe's direction, anyway. In the first, he wears khakis and a Serengeti National Park shirt. Two monkeys perch atop his shoulders. After a quick Google search you learned that last summer he worked as a safari guide in Tanzania. You hope he isn't a vegan; you dated one of those once. The whole dinner the guy eyed your plate with a look one reserves for clogged toilets.

In his second photo he dons a tuxedo; he links arms with a girl in a wedding dress who's a female version of him. According to his social media, he and his twin sister studied at the same university, and her husband was his fraternity brother. You stalked the sister's page, too. She's an equestrian and graduated from the top veterinary program in the country. She reminds you of the girls your foster mother urged you to emulate, but those girls pelted you with brown paper bags in the cafeteria.

Your phone buzzes. *Just arrived. Let me know when you're here :)* He can wait a couple minutes. You switch back to his profile. The third photo is a selfie. He's handsome in an obvious way, chiseled jaw and eyes like a verdant countryside. He looks like a hybrid of seven other guys you dated, but what earned him your right swipe was his hair. You only date blonds.

You had a great love once. That man was your sun. The air you breathed. The blood in your veins. You still gaze at the photos under your mattress. He was perfect. You still sleep in his old football t-shirts and replay his voicemails like a lullaby; you imagine his velvet voice transcending your recordings and asking for you back. You conjure him so vividly — from his shaggy blond hair to the birthmark on his left cheek — it feels like he's there. As if he never left. Some mornings you think it was all a bad dream. But then you remember you're forbidden to contact him and have no information how.

The moon hovers in your rear-view mirror. Crescent tonight. *Awesome, be there in 5* you text back. Punctuation smiley faces aren't your thing. Not that it matters what your thing is, because your thing can be whatever you want. *You* can be whatever you want, and men can't perform the ubiquitous pre-date social media autopsy because you don't exist on social media. You haven't since The Breakup. The only truth your dates have is your first name, and that's all you ever give.

Who will you be tonight?

Certainly not an orphan. Or a stalker. A threat. Sociopath. Whatever else the restraining order pegs you as. You usually curate your life based around that of your date's, so perhaps tonight you will be a twin. You've always wanted an identical sister. You two could've pranked all the kids in your foster home. Maybe tonight you'll have a pet snake. Last week you had two pet squirrels and a hedgehog.

You adjust the ruby heart dangling from your neck, the last Valentine's Day gift from your love. Sometimes you incorporate it into your fictitious life. You've said you inherited the necklace from your baroness great grandmother; your father is a jeweler and he created it for your sixteenth birthday; it was a souvenir from vacation in Aruba; you found it in a Manhattan taxicab at 3AM. Tonight you'll say you bought matching necklaces while you and your twin studied abroad in Greece.

You hop out of your car and saunter to the restaurant. Your date is probably waiting for your arrival at the bar, debating whether he should go for a handshake or a hug. People are predictable. The host will escort you two to the table and he'll start with small talk, either a comment about the weather or he'll inquire about your day. That'll be the segue into asking if you worked and if so what do you do, to if you went to school and if so where and what did you study, to your long-term goals to your hobbies to if you're watching any shows on Netflix.

When he speaks, you will listen. You will ask questions. He will feel seen. He will feel heard. Your charm will mesmerize him like a child at Fourth of July fireworks. He'll be so enamored he won't even have thought about sleeping with you, and when he walks you to your car he'll say it's been a while since he felt this excited after a first date. You'll blush, and when he asks to see you again, you'll tell him you'd like that.

But that's the last he will hear from you again.

Just walked in you text as you enter, spotting his blond hair at the dim bar. You chirp his name and he turns. His eyes light up like a fresh lamp bulb. He walks in your direction, smiling shyly when he approaches.

"Hi," you say, beaming. "I'm thrilled to meet you."

44 *Little Man, Quito, Ecuador - Roger Camp*

Sophistication

by Faith Noelle

I stare out the window, a wistful sigh dangling off my chapped lips. From forty-four floors above the ground, the tiny people look like little ants – ants scurrying about in their heels and skirts and suits, ants with their solid-colored briefcases and someplace important to be. Ants with long cigarettes placed just so between their middle and forefinger as they breathe out thick clouds of smoke. Ants who are glorious in their sophistication.

Cal stands on the other side of the room, finishing the buttons on his own suit jacket. In mere minutes he will become one of the tiny ants, dressed up nicely so that he can intimidate his coworkers and stand in front of people in an important meeting and explain a chart full of facts and figures that will help make his company a lot of money. His coworkers will pat him on the back, and then they will go outside to smoke to-gether, their own cigarettes held just so between their fingers, and then he will go home to his wife. I wonder if she is out there now, walking down the street with the other tiny ants. She is probably wearing tall heels so that after Cal finishes at his job she can come to him and greet him with a kiss, and neither one will have to bend down to reach the other. Not like Cal has to do with me. He always has to bend down to kiss me, and he complains often of his neck. His wife probably kisses him with smooth lips that are never chapped. She probably wears red lip-stick, the expensive kind. Suddenly I am flooded with a strong desire to wear red lipstick.

"Will you go shopping today?" I ask Cal.

He jerks his head up like a startled baby deer, eyes widen-ing as if only just realizing that I was in the room.

"Shopping?" He says the word like it is foreign on his tongue. "Why do you ask?"

I tell him that I want red lipstick. He looks at me as

though I am insane. Maybe I am. No one but he and I will ever see me wear it, but I want to be pretty. I stride over to the full-length mirror that sits in the corner of the room. I slowly move around in a circle, examining myself. My feet are bare and calloused, the feet of a girl growing up in a poor farm town, a girl who wore the same shoes her mother wore as a little girl. Cal's feet are smooth. They are hairy and cold when they brush against my legs, but they are feet that have known the warmth of plush carpets in the early morning and the protection of fancy leather shoes with wingtips. I would like shoes with wingtips.

My arms and legs are skinny, and quite ashy. Cal wears a melon flavored body butter that makes his skin shine, and he always smells the way I imagine a tropical island would. Cal, of course, has been to many tropical islands. I cannot say the last time I have left this apartment. I cannot say the next time I ever will. I like sitting in the window. I like to see what the people do outside, even if they are small like ants. They are very beautiful, very sophisticated ants.

Cal wears a lazy smirk as he walks over and wraps his hands around my waist. I only wear my panties and one of his old, forgotten t-shirts, so his fingers are dangerously close to bare skin. He teases the hem of my shirt and plants a trail of kisses on my neck.

"Whatever you want, babe."

My skin tingles where his lips have brushed, and I curse the way my heart flutters. Once upon a time I would curse myself because it felt wrong to get pleasure from a man who only kept me around for his own selfish games. Now I curse myself for wanting something I knew I'd have to wait for. Cal has work. The suit and tie and wing-tipped shoes mean no morning fun.

I head back to the window once Cal leaves. Most of my waking hours are spent people-watching. I eat, for Cal always makes sure there is food for me, and I clean myself if the mood hits. Mostly I just watch. I like to have the window open and to sit with one leg dangling over the edge. It pumps my blood, a dizzying rush to think that I am up so high, so precariously balanced on the line between life and death. I did this once when Cal was in the room. He had yelled and then held me close while he cried, and then he yelled some more. I no longer do this when he is in the apartment, but I know that he is not foolish enough to believe that I have stopped. I am always careful. I am not stupid.

I want to open the window today, but it is the middle of December and already freezing in the apartment. The heat does not work very well. I should remind Cal when he returns.

I decide to search through Cal's closet for an old coat or something to wear. I know he will not mind. He always smiles when he sees me wearing his clothes.

I don't find a coat. Instead I find something even better.

The bag contains the most beautiful dress I have ever laid eyes on. It is long and purple and made of silk or some such fancy material. I don't think twice before stripping myself of the shirt and slipping into the gown. I am unable to hold in the gasp as I transform from an ugly duckling into a goddess. The gown has a long slit up the side that makes me feel sexy. A pair of golden heeled sandals give me new height, and the ensemble is complete with the most wonderful mink coat that has ever existed. I may not have much to compare it to, but I know that these are the clothes worn by people in Heaven. My hair is limp and lifeless, but I can easily imagine a halo of curls around my head. I purse my lips and meet my reflection in the mirror. All that I need is red lipstick.

I grab a straw from out of the bathroom cabinet and hold it between my middle and forefingers. I bring it to my lips and pretend to blow out a ring of smoke. I was so beautiful. I was sophisticated.

I was also parading around in clothes that weren't mine. I reached into the bag to pull out a small card with Cal's familiar scribble. '*Happy anniversary*,' it reads. '*I love you, Elle, and today I'm going to make you feel like a princess. You deserve it.*'

Elle must be his wife's name. I am playing in her clothes.

I wonder if she would want them if she knew that they were currently being worn by Cal's whore. In some ways, I have won. I live with Cal, although I never leave. Brought to this city at eighteen, yet I've never really explored it. I have his body. It is a nice body, and it will have to be enough. If I believe that I am happy here, then I will be happy here.

I spin around in Elle's dress once more. She may have his heart, but tonight, I am the princess.

Judy Bowler

by Paul Smith

I hadn't been to a laundromat in a while. I knew where one was, though, about a mile from our house. It was right near Church Street where it crossed Niles Center Road, in a grim-looking strip mall alongside a Thai restaurant, a nail salon, and a medical supply store. We had a bedspread that wouldn't fit in our washer or our dryer, so off I went on a Saturday morning. Laundromats were usually dismal and depressing, but I had met girls there. Sometimes I had even looked forward to doing laundry for that reason. That was long past. Now I wanted to get this chore done ASAP.

The Thai restaurant was already cooking up some spicy stuff, and the aroma wafted out onto Church Street. I felt sorry for anyone desperate enough to eat here, seeking exotic food in our corner of this Chicago suburb. I pulled open the laundromat door, dragged in our bedspread and had a look around. Washers lined one wall, dryers the other. I wondered what they cost. An attendant was in back at a table where she sorted clothes. Overhead a sign read 'CHANGE, DETERGENT.' She was Polish-looking, with a knot of blonde hair that looked like a haystack. She was my age, when others still looked to be firm to the touch. Nobody else was there. I got a roll of quarters and some Tide. When I handed her my money, she grunted.

It turned out that the big washers cost five dollars. I remember them costing twenty- five cents. But I needed the super large washer for the bedspread. The smaller ones?

"How much for one of these?" I asked the *zaftig* attendant.

She held up two fingers and mouthed the word 'two.' I assume she meant two dollars. I smiled. Then I settled in to wait for my wash. I should have brought something to read. I fumbled in my pocket and found that roll of quarters and started looking at them. Sometimes I like to look at the dates on coins and remember what I was doing that year. The roll had a lot of the newer quarters with inscriptions of the fifty states or the national parks. I wanted the ones before that, when life had more fun in it. I found several that made me smile when the door opened. In walked a girl with a hamper of laundry, her eyes scanning the place like mine did. Our eyes touched briefly. She immediately averted them to avoid any possible connection with this man old enough to be her father, this man fumbling with a roll of quarters and giving her the once over. It seemed to me like she was new here, had not done her laundry here before. She was looking around to 'see how the place worked.' That knowledge was in my approach once upon a time. Her eyes went to the washers.

"Two dollars," I said to her. Her eyebrows went up. She nearly smiled. I looked away. She plunked some quarters in a machine with a sign above it that read 'No sitting on the washers.' She sat down in one of the few chairs near the entrance as I went back to my quarters.

I'd met a really nice girl at a laundromat out of town. Her name was the same as the Hungarian name for their country – Hungary. Then I blew it, dating her and getting caught with another girl. Quarters with that year were hard to find. I met another girl in the basement of our apartment building by the coin- operated machines. Technically, it wasn't really a laundromat because we already had something in common – living in the same building. Her name was Marcia. I dated her until I married my present wife. There was yet another girl I sort of met at a laundromat at Wrightwood and Halsted. Her name was Judy Bowler. She had a nice smile and, in retrospect, I can remember the entire make-up of her persona was to shun creatures like me without being too snotty. She listened to whatever nonsense I said and artfully deflected my advances. I remember leaving the place with a clean sack of laundry and the feeling that I'd played a chess game to a tie. Now that my washing was done here on Church Street, I surreptitiously walked back to the attendant's table where some shirts were getting sorted.

I had already started checking out the dryers. There were two kinds – Huebsch dryers and Speed Queens. Both sets looked old. I asked the lady which was better.

"Huebsch," she said, holding up one finger. I think that meant they were Number One in her book. She smiled, though. It was the kind of smile I'd seen before on Milwaukee Avenue, serving up a pierogi, driving a van around our neighborhood with a 'Kula Maids' banner on it. We had spoken twice now. We were like old friends. I went back to the washers and my quarters. When the spin cycle ended I took my clothes out and put them in one of the Huebsch dryers, set it on 'high' and turned to look at the young lady sitting near the entrance. She was doing what Judy Bowler had done, only in neutral. She didn't have to say anything, so she made a point of reading the signs on the pale blue walls 'No sitting on the washers,' 'No rugs in the front load washers,' 'Not responsible for damage and lost coins.' I got it. She could have been my daughter. I pretended to distract myself by looking at the serial numbers on the Huebsch dryers to see if they were all in sequence. They weren't. I saw 165488, then 165489, then 165495. That made me wonder the same way I wondered about the dates on the quarters. Every year or so I'd done something really stupid, something that set me back financially or in matters involving women, and yet, over the years, I never seemed to learn. After Janice Magyar, I still blundered. It was the same way with the Huebsch dryers. They should have stayed in sequence, but didn't. Something, maybe fate, or someone, maybe some sloppy equipment in-staller had gotten them mixed up and now they would never be in sequence. The young lady looked up once more. Our eyes touched. She wanted to know which dryer was better – the Huebsch or the Speed Queen.

"Huebsch," I said, looking her in the eye.

She nearly smiled again. Then her eyes went to the floor. She cleaned out the front load washer and put the whole mess into her hamper and walked out the door. She had a cute walk. She loaded her bag into a SUV and drove off. The sun had come out. It was a nice Saturday morning. The aroma of those Thai Dragon Peppers next door slipped into the laundromat and tantalized my nostrils. I heard the sound of my Huebsch dryer drop down to nothing and went to check the bedspread.

Dry.

There is something about leaving a place and person with whom you have had a small amount of interaction. Everybody handles it differently. Say you are at a basketball game and at half-time you ask the guy behind you to look at his program to see the height of the team's center. When the game is over with, it's not necessary to say 'so long' or 'nice talking to you' or 'have a good one.' But in the larger scheme of things, even in something as miniscule as this, it is imperative to say something to anoint, to hallow this social contract with the decency of a 'good-bye' because both of you are human and deserve the respect of acknowledging each other in addition to your backsides sharing an hour on the same wooden bleachers. In honor of this, in the celebration of the fact that the laundromat attendant and I had partaken some of this Saturday morning together, and also the aroma of whatever those Thai folks were cooking, I lifted my hand up as I made my way out and said, "Good-bye!"

She looked up from the piles of clothes she was sorting. A full smile came to her face, a radiant ray of sunshine straight from Warsaw with a cheerful, "Bye!"

And she held up two fingers in the symbol of a 'V.'

Smothered

by J. Ian Bush

He heard somebody telling somebody else about some woman in New Boston who smothered her baby. He knew smothered was bad because the person telling looked sour and the person listening frowned and shook her head. But he thought smothered sounded pretty and soft like pillow or blanket. He asked his mother what it meant. She asked him why he wanted to know. So, he told her about how the person told the other person about the woman in New Boston who smothered her baby. She told him that smothering was a bad thing that makes it so you can't breathe. He knew that if you don't breathe you die. Surely nobody would want to make a baby dead. Old people die and people get sad, but it's okay because they're old and they've had time. Babies are new and need time to get old. He never saw a dead person before. Besides on TV. But that isn't real. Those are actors and they die a lot and have all kinds of different names. He thought maybe the woman in New Boston didn't know that smothering was a bad thing because it's such a soft word.

King Merneptah's Hands
by Maev Barba

It is not feasible after a battle to make soldiers count.

It is not feasible to make a scribe wander aimlessly through a battlefield.

Soldiers cut hands off the bodies, one hand per body, and arrange them in a grid for scribes to tally.

Two hands; two dead. Five hands; five dead. A thousand hands; a thousand dead.

Rows and columns of hands thumb-to-pinky and tip-to-heel.

Three-hundred hands widthwise, two-hundred hands length: altogether, six thousand men dead.

Merneptah's men piled the hands in carts and rolled them back to Memphis.

Entering through white gates of stone, hands trembling in their carts, the soldier's wives came picking through the fingers.

How do we know you've won a war and that these are not the hands of other wives?

Merneptah ordered his men to stop. They upended their carts and hands spilled out into the streets.

Then they turned around and marched back to the battlefield.

Finally, by nightfall, they returned, carts not trembling with hands, but jiggling with penises.

Love at First Sight, Every Morning

by David Schwartz

Love at first sight. It's the story and stuff of my adult life. The first time I looked at him, I didn't just love the way he looked. I loved the way he looked at me. His intense gaze showed he wanted to know the real me; to care for and to possess me. He stared at me with an urgency that made me breathless, awed, dizzy, hot, wet, and happy beyond comprehension. I literally didn't want to blink, to take away his visual caress.

When he smiled, I saw a facial expression before me I had never known existed. It said: "I'm so vulnerable that I will not take you seriously if I have the slightest reason to think you might hurt me." Then, as we moved to the small dance floor, I caught another first sight: the mirrors reflected golden sunlight coming through the skylight. The image of the two of us looked just perfect. He was too short for me and I was too pudgy for his skinny frame, and yet I thought we were in Divine light; that there was simply no other couple on earth more beautiful than we were.

What looks like a whirlwind courtship to those on the outside feels like a life-altering communion to the couple having that courtship; what seems "too fast" to others is experienced as 'at last' to the lovers. So, it was with my man and me.

The tender intimate fantasy in his eyes (yes, call it ogling) was more than flattering: it took my breath away. It still does.

Unblinking

by Jonathan van Belle

Part I: A severed head with its eyelids cut off.

The floating mass, rounded by gravity, orbiting a star, hosted billions of little organisms that named themselves *human*. They received our gift.

Part II: Pandemic

From onset to death, it requires one to five days. The average time is three days and twelve hours. The medium of the Jolly Jolly's transmission, RTCD-N9, was unknown to these organisms. The duration from the first kill to the final kill was 42 days. Result: all organisms killed.

Part III: The Jolly Jolly

Per your request, Suzerain Xqr, a poetic reenactment for your children:

Bodies, ejaculate of God, sore and flush, fell dreaming.
Dreaming of our gift, unblinking, staring, unblinking, screaming
At them, at all times, all places.
Unsleeping, none could look away;
In any direction they lidless too became in all swimming pain.

The Jolly Jolly's neck bled every second, the jolly horror unblinking
In every eye: those in love could see no more each other's faces,
Screamed their desperate love through the Jolly Jolly's scream.
Screaming all, one by one, to reach beyond jolly hateful lidless
eyes:
"Help!"

Part IV: Hope

The floating mass is clean. The head moves on to the next. Breathe easy. Send my love.

Third Party
by Gale Acuff

At Miss Hooker's funeral I'll fall in
love with her all over again, red hair
and green eyes and freckles and her eyes closed
like they used to be when she recited
the Lord's Prayer at the end of Sunday
School class and I peeked to see how she looked

with them closed, maybe asleep or resting
them and now she's dead. I never touched her
but I always wanted to even though
I'm 10 to her 25 but now that
she's gone I'm not sure how old she is
or when her soul will soar to Heaven, I

must've missed that class, whether it must wait
inside her body until Judgment Day
or if it jumps free as soon as she dies
choking on a bone at the Korn Dawg King.
I'll wish I could've been there to save her,
to pry her lips apart, they sure look sweet,

and reach down deep into her throat and pull
it out, the bone I mean, or push it down
into her belly, I'm no doctor but
I think my fingers would've seen for my
eyes. Everyone would've cried, You saved her,
and when she gets back on her feet she'll say

Oh thank you, Gale - my, that was a close one
and now you're my hero, and of course she'll
kiss me, but on the cheek I guess and not
the lips, which I can understand because
we'll both be embarrassed, and then she'll fall
in love with me even though she's fifteen

years older but she'll wait until I was
legal, 16 I guess but she'll find out,
and then invite me to her place for some
coffee maybe, which I don't drink but I'll
learn, or pie and ice cream, I like apple,
the pie I mean, and prefer my ice cream

chocolate, and the pie should be piping
hot and the ice cream almost frozen so
that when she puts a scoop (or three) on top
it's like Heaven coming to grips with Hell
or matter with antimatter and it
explodes into something spectacular

like sweet romance. I'll tell Miss Hooker, Oh,
I just did what anybody would do,
even though they didn't, they panicked but
I was cool and saved the woman I love
and for my reward God gives her to me
to have and to hold and so on and so

forth. But then she'll be dead so she won't know
how I feel, not that she felt the same but
I figure she's gone and her soul's in
Heaven, I mean if it doesn't have to
hang in the grave until Judgment Day, so
she's where God is and since I say my prayers

every night before I go to bed
and since she's On High or in God's general
area then maybe she'll overhear
and then she'll feel better about being
dead and maybe she'll answer my prayers
or at least give me a sign she's listening -

she could come to me in a dream or as
an angel. I think she'd look good in wings.
Or I'll wake up one morning to find on
my other pillow a lock of her red
hair, or I'll look in the mirror and one
of my eyes, or maybe both, will be green

or I'll see freckles popping up. When they

lower Miss Hooker into her resting
place maybe I'll cry Stop! - the way they do
on TV when some couple's getting spliced

but a third party objects. But I'll keep
my mouth shut while they sprinkle dirt on top

and then they use a shovel and then I'll
split with it still not filled in but later
some guy with a Bobcat will do it or
that's what I would do, I'll make Miss Hooker
as comfortable as I can while she's
dead until it hurts. It hurts already.

San Francisco

by Sunset Combs

And I sat down on the pier, the lights from the city I had only just met shining on the water like false sunlight. Sea lions slept in drying piles on swaying docks. A few of them wailed, a chortle or a war cry that echoed on air. Two in the back, visible only from their outlines and the silver streaks of shine on their wet coats, opened their mouths and moved toward each other. And I thought of you. They wiggled and they taunted and in the midst of their spat or their dance, they flopped into the water, dropping into black disappearance. After only a moment, one slipped through the surface and climbed back on the dock, drifting but chained. The other stayed below or surfaced elsewhere in the shadows unseen. And I watched the lone sea lion that reappeared squirm on its back, trying to right itself; trying to meet belly with wood and sleep. And I thought of you. The night was only slightly cold, the chill I always crave with darkness. I sat, the smell of fish now familiar, and I watched. The sea lion turned, the sigh after struggle, and it relaxed into the rocking wood. And I thought of you. I left when my can was empty, my feet sore from running toward the sound of singing sea lions, and I knew how far away you were and that I could not run to you. That once I had not wanted to. I walked back toward the tram, a sudden content exhaustion settling into the wind that whipped me, and I thought: if I could slip through the water, if I could emerge, if I could run to you, would I?

A Warm September in Arizona

by Phoebe Glen

Months leading up to the big event were filled with Chile Rellenos and
  The Simpsons reruns.

I woke up, just like any other day, and began to get ready for school.

Then Mom said, "You can't go to school today. Your sister is in labor."

As we rushed to the Birthing Clinic, I had no idea what was in
store for the day.

By the end of it, we would journey on a "rollercoaster of
emotions" together.

When we arrived, they took you to your room and prepared the bath.

Whether you would have a water birth was yet to be determined.

To think you had been in labor all through the night was hard for
me to grasp.

As the final hours approached, I watched you morph into an
animal, desperate to
get your baby out...naturally.

First the Doctor broke your water.

I held your hand and told you to keep pushing.

Even when you said you could not do it anymore,
I encouraged you and cheered you on,
"You can do this. Keep going!"

Then the moaning.
Next the crowning.

Then she cut.

And finally, he arrived.
Your beautiful baby boy, flapped his arms like a bird's wings.
It was amazing!
I was terrified, but also overcome with a feeling of euphoria.

A bond we will always share.

A love beyond measure.

A reason to live.

Family.

The Golem of Prague
by Z.B. Wagman

1592 - The Holy Roman Empire, Prague

A sharp knocking jarred Judah from his deep slumber. The darkness outside his window did little to reassure him. He was much too old for midnight visitors. "What is it?" he called, his voice choked with the grit of sleep.

"Maharal!" called a familiar voice as the handle to his front door rattled. "Maharal, I have news."

Blinking back the sleep, he placed the voice: young Philipp. It was enough to get Judah to push back the too-thin blankets and climb to his feet. As the knocking came again, Judah fumbled for his cane and pulled a robe from the back of a nearby chair. He could not move as fast as he once did. The knocking came again before he was halfway across the front room. "Patience," he rasped as he stumbled to the door. "Patience, please."

As soon as Judah lifted the latch, the door swung outward to reveal a young man—a boy really, Philipp could not have been more than twenty. By the light of a flickering lantern, Judah could see that the boy's clothes were sharp and vibrant, a stark contrast to the Maharal's threadbare robe. More importantly the boy had forgone his badge. Only this youth would dare leave off the six-pointed star that the rest of them were forced to wear. But it was not the missing badge that caught the Maharal's eye. It was the boy's face. He was frantic and slick with sweat, even on such a cold night. He must have run straight from the palace.

Philipp spoke before the Maharal could marshal his thoughts. "It's happened again, Rabbi. They've found another one."

The Maharal found himself lacking in words. Either sleep

or age was clouding his mind. "I see," he finally said before turning back into his home. "Come. You must tell me all."

The youth eased into the room, shutting the door behind him. The lantern light revealed a small dining room with a potbellied stove in the corner. "Please," Judah said, his voice still graveled by sleep. "See to the fire."

"But—" The boy began to protest but Judah cut him off, taking the lantern from his hand and setting it on the table.

"Your news can wait until we are settled. Don't leave an old man to shiver on this cold night."

The boy sighed but knelt in front of the old iron stove. As the boy worked, Judah filled the teapot from his basin. He returned the tin pot to the top of the stove and settled into the chair closest to the stove. Philipp rose, a fire crackling merrily in the hearth, and perched on the chair across from the rabbi.

"Alright Philipp, tell me what has brought you to my home in the middle of the night."

"They found another kid, Rabbi. A girl this time."

"And where did they find her?"

"Down by the river. Not far from here."

"I see." It was unsettling news, though not wholly unexpected. "When did they find her?"

"Not an hour ago. I overheard them telling the emperor and ran straight here."

The Maharal did not ask what the youth was doing in the emperor's chambers so late at night. The emperor's proclivities were a wide-open secret. And, as this meeting proved, it paid to have someone in the lap of power. "Do they suspect anyone?"

Philipp shook his head. "It's like the others. No witness, no leads. One of the night's-watch practically stumbled over her while on his rounds."

"And we can expect much the same response as we saw with the others." This was the fifth such child to be found this month. All found with their throats slit. All found near the Jewish quarters. "Thank you for bringing this to me Philipp. We must expect a difficult time ahead of us."

"What are you going to do?"

"Right now? I'm going back to sleep."

"What?!" Philipp spluttered. "Back to sleep? But Rabbi—"

"There's nothing to be done 'til morning," the old man said with a deep sigh.

"But I ran all this way."

"And I've thanked you for it." Judah stood, his cane shaking with exertion as he did. "But there's nothing I can do this night. I must be prepared for the harsh light of morning. It will be a hard day for all of us."

"But—"

"The best way I can prepare," Judah continued, raising his voice over the boy. "Is by getting sleep. You could do the same. Please now, leave me to prepare."

Philipp rose and made his way to the door. "I…I'm sorry if I disturbed you. I just thought…" He trailed off as he undid the latch.

"You did well, Philipp." Judah said, his rough voicing smoothed. "You do not realize, perhaps, how much you have helped."

The young man turned and met the Maharal's gaze. With a small nod, he stepped out into the night.

Judah sighed, letting the mantle of the Maharal drop from him. Too soon he would have to pick it back up again. He turned and plodded over to the stove where the tea water hummed in a boil. With a shaking hand he removed it and poured into a waiting mug.

* * *

By midmorning the entire city had heard of the girl's death. The markets raged with the news. "We cannot let this go on," one preacher cried from atop his soapbox. His stark white robes placed him as more than just a street-side sermonizer. "The emperor will not speak out but we know the truth. We know where the darkness lies in this city." He stood in the square that divided the jewish quarters from the rest of town. As he spoke a crowd began to gather and the Maharal was quick to note that not a single one of them wore a six-pointed badge.

The Maharal had made a point to be out amongst his people this morning. As he walked the alleys of the ghetto many a person stopped to ask if the news was true. Everybody knew what a dead child meant. Especially a dead Christian one. The Maharal stopped and spoke soothing words to any who would hear. He tried to calm their frayed nerves; to focus his people on the comfort that tomorrow would bring. But when he got to the market he was not surprised to find this preacher undoing his careful work.

"Our city has suffered enough at the grubby hands of these leeches. It is time to cast them out." The preacher's vehemence was rubbing off on the crowd. With every hate-filled stanza, the Maharal could see violence forming in the thoughts of those gathered. "They kill our children. They use the blood to make their bread. We all know it to be true. So it is time to act. For our children's safety if not for our own!"

These were claims that the Maharal had heard all his life. Always from someone like this priest. He would not listen to them again. He stepped forward, intent on soothing the gathered mob, but someone else spoke first. "Who are you to accuse us? We have done nothing wrong." The speaker was standing across the gathering from the Maharal. He was a tall man, one who wore his badge with pride: Rafal Levitsky, the baker's eldest.

"I am Vladamir Prucha, abbot of Strahov Monastery and

companion to the emperor. And you are a Jew who has not been shown his place."

"Worse than you have tried," Rafal yelled back. But the crowd bristled and, as if commanded, reached for the man. As the first blows rained down upon the man, the Maharal could hear others trying to come to his aid. If he did not act more than blows would be traded. But what to do? As he turned, he caught sight of the abbot. A grin had slid its way onto the preacher's face. A grin not of amusement, but of calculation.

Judah spun, catching sight of the red and gold uniforms of watchmen. Stumping over to them as fast as his cane would allow, Judah reached out a shaking hand to one. "Do something," he wheezed. But from the grin on the man's face he knew that it was no good.

"About what?" The man barked, not taking his eyes off the melee.

"They're killing him."

"They'll only rough him up," the guard's companion said with a snicker. "And if they do well… it wouldn't be much of a loss."

Judah cast his eyes about the market, trying to find something that would put an end to the carnage. But all he saw was ruin. Carts were overturned, stalls abandoned, and the people—his people—had scattered. All those left were intent on harm. Judah shook his head, turning away from the square, and wiped the water from his eyes. He left the two guards, still laughing, behind. There was nothing an eighty year-old man could do in the face of such violence. Or at least, almost nothing.

* * *

The ghetto was deathly quiet for the rest of the afternoon. Anyone who could, stayed off the streets. Those who couldn't hastened along, casting fugitive glances over their shoulders. Rafal was not the only one to lose their life to that morning's butchery. Moshe Lesky and Suzzana Catz also fell to the mob's fists as they tried to help Rafal. The chevra kadisha was busy that afternoon preparing the bodies for burial.

The Maharal sent feelers out into the non-Jewish corridors of Prague. What he heard was not promising. Most of the city saw the deaths as retribution, a sort of payment for the children who had died. But their anger was far from slaked. To make matters worse, Abbot Prucha continued to spread his blood libel around the city. Philipp reported that after the mob had dissipated, the abbot had visited the palace. The emperor had granted him a private audience which not even Philipp could find what it was about. Whatever it was did not dissuade the abbot from spreading his hatred. His monks swept throughout the city. It seemed every marketplace and street corner now acted as pulpit to a radical in white.

"We should go."

The Maharal had gathered the leaders of the community together in his front room. For three hours the wealthy and influential had been crammed around his dinner table. There was Rabbi Openheim, the Maharal's successor at the Altneuschul; Mordechai Maisel, the philanthropist who had built one of Prague's most beautiful synagogues; Betzel Gershom, a printer and leader amongst the younger Jews; and of course Philipp, the emperor's favorite.

Rabbi Openheim was the leading voice in an argument that they were all too familiar with. "Maybe Anatolia will take us. We've done it before and, if it means safety for our people, we should do it again."

Judah caught the eye of Mordechai from across the room. They were both old enough to remember what it had been like thirty years ago when they had been forced out. And again, twenty years before that. It was not an experience they would choose to repeat. But, though the rabbi was not old enough to remember, he had a point. The city in those days had felt similar. As if it were a hive buzzing with anticipation. And Judah was afraid that this Abbot Prucha was just the man to break it open.

"The bloodshed will continue," the rabbi said, looking about the room for support. "And there's nothing we can do to stop it."

"So we fight back." Betzel stood up, pushing his chair back from the table with force. "If they want bloodshed, we can give it to them."

"No," the Maharal said, cutting across the youth. "Too many have been killed already."

"But Rabbi—"

"No. I will not see more young people die in a fruitless cause."

"But what other choice is there?" Betzel persisted. "If we leave, people will die too. Do you think my mother can make such a journey? Even you, Maharal, can you truly claim to be able to survive a journey of hundreds of miles?"

The Maharal sighed. "No. I do not claim such power."

"Then why shouldn't we fight?" Betzel had allowed himself to get worked up. His voice was raised in accusation. "If we stay, people die. If we have to die, why shouldn't it be while fighting for our home?"

"Because the emperor won't let you." Philipp's voice was cool as he stared across the table at Betzel. "The moment you fight back, Rudolf will bring his army down on the ghetto like a fist. He will smash all of your resistance and burn this place to the ground. We are lucky he has not done so already."

"What do you mean?" Asked Mordechai, the old man leaning forward in his chair. "What has been said?"

"Rudolf has hinted that he is feeling pressure to exert more power over us."

"That's no big surprise," the Maharal said, leaning back in his chair.

"No," Philipp agreed. "But I think Rudolf is strongly considering it."

"All the more reason to leave then," Rabbi Openheim cut in. "We need to go before the emperor is forced to act."

The Maharal raised a hand, silencing the younger rabbi. He found Philipp's eyes across the table. "Can you go to him? Can you talk him down?"

The youth paused to consider. "Maybe. The abbot is hard pressed against us. But I think Rudolf will listen."

"What if we removed the abbot?" Betzel cut in. "Without him, surely the populace would calm down."

"Only after burning a dozen of us in recompense."

It was enough to cool Bezel's fury. "So what then…we leave?"

"Let me see what I can do," Philipp said, raising to his feet. "Give me a couple of days and then we can decide."

* * *

For the second night in a row, Judah found himself being awoken in the middle of the night by someone pounding on his door.

"What is it?" Judah grumbled as he threw open the door. A boy, a young one, whimpered and thrust a scrap of paper into the Maharal's hand. Before Judah could say anything more, the boy turned and scampered into the night. He shook his head and turned back into his home. There were few places the messenger could have come from at this time of night. With shaking hands he lit his candle. By the dim light he could barely make out the handwriting on the note.

They've found another one.

Rudolf's sending troops in the morning.

-p

Judah collapsed into the nearest chair. It was all moving too fast. They needed more time. His eyes began to sting. It had been a long time since he had felt so powerless. His people were counting on him and he had let them down. If only he had tried harder. If only he had more power. If only…

He raised his head out of his hands. With a burst of strength he took hold of his cane and pushed himself to his feet. Rushing as fast as his frail body would allow, he retreated to his bedroom where he kept his most prized tomes. Even without his candles' meager light he knew which one he wanted. It was his oldest, most ragged volume. Rumors said it was centuries old. And it might just hold the answers that they so desperately needed.

* * *

As the first warming rays of morning touched the city a company of troops emblazoned with the yellow and black Imperial eagle poured into the market square. A slight breeze was all that moved throughout the rest of the ghetto. Any other day and there might be children in the streets and pedestrians enjoying the crisp air. But today doors remained locked and families hid. More than one face was already covered in tears.

Only two forms stood against the ugliness that was about to unfold. In the center of the market, an old man leaned stiffly on his cane. There was little hope as he looked at the gathered soldiers. His robes were ratty and covered in muck. And he looked as if the cane were the only thing keeping him on his feet. Behind him a figure loomed. It must have been ten feet tall. It stood at attention stiffer than any of the soldiers across the square.

"Clear the area!" A sergeant barked at the two figures. "By order of His Holy Roman Emperor; the King of Hungary, Croatia, and Bohemia; the Archduke of Austria, Rudolf the Second."

Neither of the figures moved.

The sergeant hesitated, glancing down the ranks towards his captain. The captain sat astride a roan charger, one of the only such animals in the square. The captain nodded.

The sergeant yelled again. "By command of His Holy Roman Emperor, you are to clear the square. If you are of jewish descent you have been given until sunday to leave the city."

Still the figures did not move.

With another nod from his captain, the sergeant broke from the line and advanced towards the figures. Before he could get more than a couple of yards the old man raised his hand.

"Come no further." Though the man's voice warbled with age, the soldiers were able to make out every word. "I am Rabbi Judah Loew ben Bezalel, the Maharal of Prague. These people are under my protection. If you continue your show of force you will be stopped."

The sergeant wasn't the only one to laugh. "Oh yeah? I think we could get through you no problem, grandad."

The Maharal lowered his hand back to his cane. "It is not me you have to worry about. I leave that to my associate Yossele." With that, he turned and began to hobble back in the direction of the ghetto proper. His companion stood as rigid as ever.

The sergeant stared after the old man, baffled. To give him credit, this Yossele was a big fellow. But even such a giant couldn't stand against the hundred men gathered here.

With a word from the captain, the troops began to advance. The sergeant was one of the first to reach the giant figure. Club raised and companions at his back, the man paused one last time. "Really buddy, you don't want to do this. Go follow your grandpa and nobody has to get hurt."

Yossele didn't so much as flinch.

With a sigh and a shrug the sergeant brought his club down. A loud crack echoed across the square.

* * *

Judah stopped at the edge of the market, just out of sight of the troops. He heard the sergeant addressing Yossele. And he heard the sergeant's club snap off of the golem. He felt like he owed it to these men to watch what was about to happen. And a part of him was more than a little curious.

Then the screaming started. Once again, Judah found tears springing to his eyes.

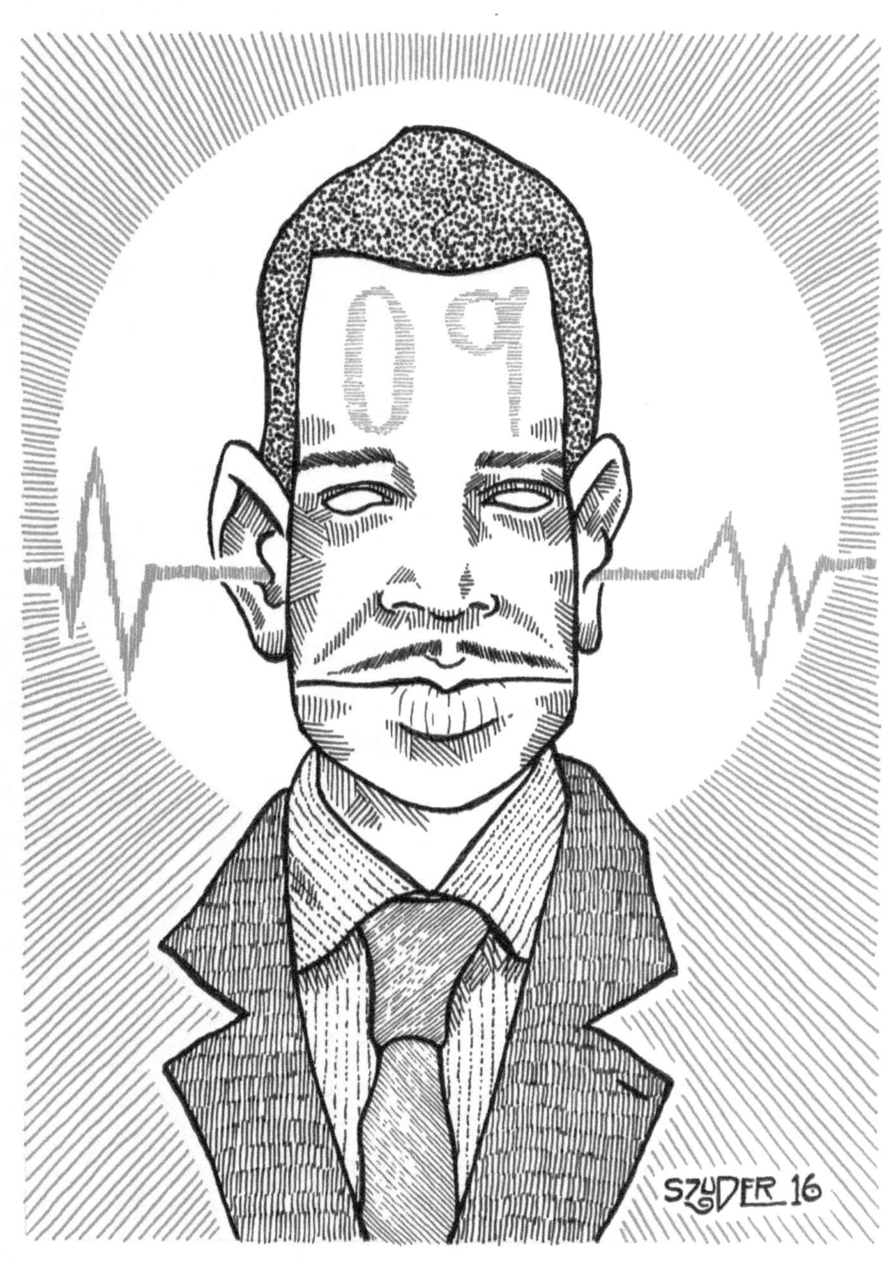

74 *Untitled - Jeremy Szuder*

Hobgob
by John Chrostek

A man is mowing his lawn at dawn with Airpods on in a yard five houses down. He is listening to a convicted felon describe fugue states and contemplating the utter silence of his street. It has been almost eight months since his wife left with Arwen, their Bichon Frise, to somewhere outside Helena somewhere buffalos roam in open fields and the air smells like lavender, grass and honey, and he has not recovered at all. He can still fear anger's searing grip on his throat. He knows he put a fist through drywall. There is a stain of wine on the white den carpet, but it is just a hole where the world fell in and left the house and his body behind.

He feels comfortable crying loudly in the quarantine. When he looks into the mirror, he sees a thing he does not recognize, a red-eyed warthog in cotton. He spends most of his hours online piloting and mining morphite as Hobgob for the Eye of Inferno corporation in EVE Online. He has contributed hundreds of real-world dollars to the EoI along with friends online, friends whose real names he has forgotten. After all, what use is a name that was unchosen? What use is a name?

Someone he trades with is a personal fitness trainer. BurrowManELO. It was him that suggested the podcast. He was also getting a divorce. He said there was little point in worrying, that no one stays together forever anymore. He said (he was drunk) that the world is an ocean and humans were fish that had just developed eyes. For the first time they could look down and see how deep and dark it all goes, like if Wile E. Coyote was born into the world above a cliff. He said it was scary, and it made sense no one could talk to each other anymore and nothing interpersonal could last. He met the guy his wife is seeing, he was a chef. He made a mean tortellini. BurrowManELO wishes them the best.

Hobgob is standing at the mirror, the mower still running in the yard. He didn't used to be a Hobgob. Once, he was a boy in a basement with a violent cousin, once he was holding a rubber brick as it was dropped in a pool. Once he was painting his neighbor's garage. At some point something shifted. He had swam too deep in the ocean of the world and disappeared. Hobgob thinks that all this is what was normal, this sunken world, and someone else had lived within him, someone who had reason to live like this up to a point and then abandon it.

She tells him Arwen's eating well, there's plenty of room for her to run. He laughs. She tells him to stay indoors, to not get sick. He feels lightheaded. He says, "We were fish that had no eyes," and wishes her well with the buffalo. He says he is doing good on his own, getting a lot done. They struggle through the rest of the call.

When the phone call ends, he walks back out into the yard. The light of the day is blinding. He climbs onto the mower and drives, covering his eyes from the light. With a scraping bump, the mower peels out into the street. Squinting, he turns off the clippers and lets it drive, rolling slowly down into the neighborhood. The limbs of the body feel loose and distant and everything is bright. The fish of a man wants nothing, can want for nothing. There is too much to the world, it is all so much, it hurts.

Empty Cupboards
by Timothy Arliss O'Brien

The desolation started during the pandemic.
Lines at the bank wrapped around and around the block.
For some
It was their first encounter with the demon of food insecurity.

The young ones cried carrying around an empty stomach for
God knows how long,
While the parents whimpered embarrassed as headlines labeled
them failures.

Others hoarded supplies as normal. More than enough to over-
flow their plates, their houses, even their silos.

The angels looked down in disgust as they counted resources,
knowing there was plenty for every hungry mouth and yearn-
ing stomach, while supplies rotted in the fields, untouched.

The seraphim begged for the creator to intervene, and stop the
destruction of His most
precious sculptures,

"I've tried, they've refused my help and won't love themselves,
each other." Was all the almighty everlasting would echo.

"If only they could share," said Saint Peter, working tirelessly at
the golden gates in the clouds, granting reprieve and entrance
to lines and lines of casualties wrapped around and around the
block.

Dead Letters
by Michael Santiago

I had become my father. Another alcoholic destined down a dark road of desperation. Rife with self-loathing, destitution, and despondency. A dissolute barfly full of contradictory, yet melancholic thoughts. My everyday was my yesterday. Nothing ever changed. Maybe because I was not ready for it to change.

So, once again, I found myself at The Maw, the dankest bar in the middle of fucking nowhere Nebraska. I was nine shots in, placing my forehead ever so gently on the edge of the bar. Mind was rattled like a birdcage, and my head was pounding. Couldn't think straight. Couldn't see straight. Suddenly, some asshole decided to slam his drink down with such vigor I shot right up, snapping me out of my hypnotized, somber state.

Glancing at the clock, I could sense that the horrid wailing of grunge would soon overcome the speakers, which were conveniently located above my head.

"Right on cue, here comes the banshees howling away," Cyrus affirmed as the music began to play.

The music blared through the busted speakers as all the "outstanding citizens" got locked into a hypnotic frenzy. Banging their heads to every thud. Slamming their fists to every scream. This scene grew tiresome by the minute and I wanted out. The music was loud enough to reanimate every corpse in the morgue two blocks from here. If for nothing more than to remind these degenerates that rest in peace meant something.

"Why the fuck do I come here? And why does this shithole play the same obnoxious band every single night," I said.

Reaching for my car keys, I pushed myself up with both palms clasped onto the stool. That final push reconfirmed that I had accomplished my mission – to reach oblivion. Stumbling

from one end of the bar to the other, I found my head sway-
ing from side to side. This was something I had gotten good
at. Getting so drunk I couldn't even feel my legs propelling me
forward. Well, the hard truth is that I wouldn't leave until I got
to this point, so part of me was cognizant to this self-inflicted,
tortuous routine.

As each hand shimmied me closer to the barkeep, the bar
seemed to stretch out further and further into eternity.

"Tony, I'll get the usual," a woman with auburn locks said.

"Double tequila sunrise?" Tony questioned.

"Hell, make it a triple tonight," she replied.

"You got it honey," he said.

How fortunate, the only thing keeping me from paying
this tab and getting the fuck out of here is this fiery headed
vixen that is impeding my path. So, I shouted, "Love, if you
wouldn't mind moving the fuck along now."

She turned towards me and began to do one of those slow
claps. You know, those claps that showed you how much of an
idiot you were. And to be frank, it sobered me up just a tiny bit.

"You're a real fucking prick, you know that?" she stated
with a cold glare.

"So, I'm told. I like to accrue these sort of accolades, you
know?" I replied with a drunken grimace.

A blatant unamused look blanketed her face. Tony handed
her a drink, and she tossed her hair back, swinging her hips as
she walked away. Admiring the curvature, she flipped me off
and joined the crowd. Still, I couldn't help but think she was
the most stunning creature in this joint.

Fixating my attention back to Tony, I shouted "How much
do I owe you?"

I opened my wallet as the proverbial moth flew right out.

Not a single dollar in sight. Destitute like my father. Just the stark, depressing reminder that I needed right now.

"Kid, you've been here every fucking night for the last two weeks in a row, and you've only paid your tab twice. You owe me so goddamn much you might as well start investing in this place. I know times are tough considering your father's passing, but you're going to have to eventually pay up. I can't keep covering you like this," Tony yelled back.

"Listen Tony, I'll pay you back. Once I get back to college, I guarantee you'll be paid before tuition," Cyrus rebutted.

"You dropped out of college months ago. Are you so gone that you forgot that? I wonder what Frank would say. Next time, I won't be so generous with letting you off the hook. You understand, kid?" he cynically replied.

There he goes. Scolding me again and reminding me how disapproving my dead father would be of my behavior. As if my dad was anyone to speak.

"Ok. Ok, Tony. I'll get the money to you as soon as I can," I reassured.

"You say that every time. And here I am, still opening shop like I'm the fucking Salvation Army. This is the last time, kid. I mean that," Tony stated as he slammed his fist into his palm.

The Maw had become an apothecary. I used this place to quench my inner turmoil. Deep down, I knew I didn't even deserve Tony's generosity, but nonetheless, he conceded because of his pity towards me. Despite the veiled threats delivered, Tony was a good man that was just looking after his friend's son in the only way he knew how, but I knew it had its limits.

Staggering towards the exit, I threw the door open and collapsed into a puddle. Spewing puke like a scene from The Exorcist. I reached for anything nearby to hold me up and stabilize me, and I began to move onward once more. With a drifting gaze, I began to hurl myself towards my car in the lot. Thankfully, vomiting had sobered me up quite a bit, which meant I might be able to drive home without fear of a DUI.

"Lady luck is finally sparing me some," I muttered.

When I reached for the car door, I saw a pile of letters bound by rubber bands next to a parked car. Grabbing them, I noticed there were quite a few of them sealed. It's as if they were meant to be delivered to someone tonight, but the person was in such a hurry it slipped their mind.

Unaware of who these letters might belong to, I grabbed them and sat in my car. Opening the first letter and pouring over every word with a burning curiosity. The interest couldn't be tamed by my intoxicated state. And so, I removed the first envelope and began reading.

This is the last letter. The final segment to this ongoing chapter. To an ongoing story that must meet its conclusion. Crippled by every breath and held back by every moment. Life is an ongoing cycle of respective movements bringing me ever closer. And tonight, the story holds no sequel. A long slumber accompanied by a lack of fear. How light carries on. Even after the final chapter. A time meant to come, yet not soon enough.

I'm sorry.

Lilith

"What the fuck am I reading. Who is Lilith? Shit, this is dated today," I said.

Then, I opened the second, then the third, and so on. These letters were dated back for several months. Clearly, someone was struggling with something so severe they saw no respite in anything. All I could feel in that moment was an intense sadness for this girl. It reminded me of my father. He, too, had left a letter behind like this after he called quits to this thing called life. Then, I began to read what seemed to be the first letter, which was obviously at the bottom of the pile.

These words may come as a shock. But I am ready to cease. My soul screams with rage. It is `tired. It cannot fathom an *existence in which this continues. I am tired. I am broken and defeated. What has happened, has happened. Who am I? I cannot change anything. Nor am I anyone to change anything. He tore what I had left out of me and crushed me. The abuse. The trauma. I've lost who I am. How long can I endure this? Not much longer.*

I'm in so much pain over so many things. It persists – day in and day out.

Lilith

"Who the fuck is Lilith? Is she at this bar? Why would she want this for herself?" I questioned.

As I teared up, I began to reminisce the day I got the call about dad. He was found dead in his garage from carbon monoxide poisoning. The news blindsided me. I knew he had spiraled into depression after mom died, and then there was him losing his job, but I didn't realize it had gotten that bad. The Maw and his house were the only places he'd frequent. If only I knew what battles he was fighting before, maybe, just maybe I could've helped him fight. The only thing left behind was a house full of memories and a note left for me.

Reaching for the door handle, I pried myself out of the driver's seat and made my way back to the bar. However, most of the cars, at this point, were out of the parking lot. I shouted for Lilith as I kicked the front door open. It appeared the denizens of the dump had already vacated.

"Tony, do you know a Lilith?" I asked.

"What the hell are you still doing here? Lilith? She left an hour ago." Tony said.

"What did she look like? Where did she go?" I responded.

Hesitating, I handed Tony the stack of letters with hope that he would pry one open to delve in. Of course, Tony being Tony, he didn't have time, and reciprocated with a dead gaze.

"I found these in the lot, and it talks about this girl, Lilith.

I spent the last hour reading every letter here," I stated.

"She's that red head you exchanged words with earlier," he insisted.

"You got to be pulling my leg, Tony," I said with a sarcastic tone.

"I ain't messing around, kid. She dipped out of here around 40 minutes ago," he confirmed.

In a panicked state, I began scribing my thoughts onto a napkin.

I have your letters. Do not follow through with whatever it is you're planning. I know the pain this leaves behind. Please reach out. I hope you get this - Cyrus

"If she happens to come back just give her this note. Do you have any idea where she might live?" I desperately asked.

"I'm not sure. Let me think. Ok, she does use a credit card to pay most nights. Let me contact the card company and report fraud to see if I can get something. But, at this hour, I'm not sure how much luck I'm gonna have. Give me a few minutes," he replied.

My eyes darted around the dim, rustic interior of The Maw. Broken bottles littered the shit stained floor, which was accompanied by the pungent smell of piss. The tiles were cracked, and the walls were peeling. For the first time in a while, I began to see the bar for what it was. A tomb. Every night, wallowing in self-blame and pity, I had to let what happened with my father go. Although not much seemed salvageable, trying to forgive was the only way forward. This had become an unexpected wake up for where my life was heading.

"Kid, I got something. 7255 Aurora Lane," Tony shouted over the phone.

Now, sobered up, a vestige of hope remained, and I scrambled towards Aurora.

Darting past every red light, the piercing howl of sirens overcame me. "Shit. Shit, not now, I don't have time for this," I muttered. Yet, the police cruiser hurled right past me. Letting out a brief sigh of relief, I was still determined.

When I arrived, Aurora was flooded with flashes of red and blue. As I slowed down, I noticed a man sitting on the front porch of 7255 with his palms covering his face. Two officers were talking to the man as he was sobbing. Then, a stretcher came out the front door, and I could see those same locks from earlier. Letting out a series of expletives, I began to slam my hands on the dashboard. My hands were trembling as I reached for the stack of letters and got out of the car.

One of the cops saw me approaching and he made his way towards me.

"I have these letters. I found them earlier at this bar she was at. They were Lilith's," I spoke softly.

"Son, I'll have to take these off you, but I'll inform the father. Wait a moment. I've got a few questions to ask," the officer responded.

"Dead letters," I whispered.

As regret overcame me, I could not help but ponder a different scenario. If the trajectory had been skewed slightly then another possible outcome could have existed. Now, a stack of dead letters is left in the wake. Just like dad.

This had to be put behind me. I had to forgive myself. I had to remind myself that not everyone can be saved, but that I could still save myself. This drunken routine had to cease. I had to free myself from the burden of what my father did. It seemed impossible. But after tonight, I was determined. I couldn't end up this way.

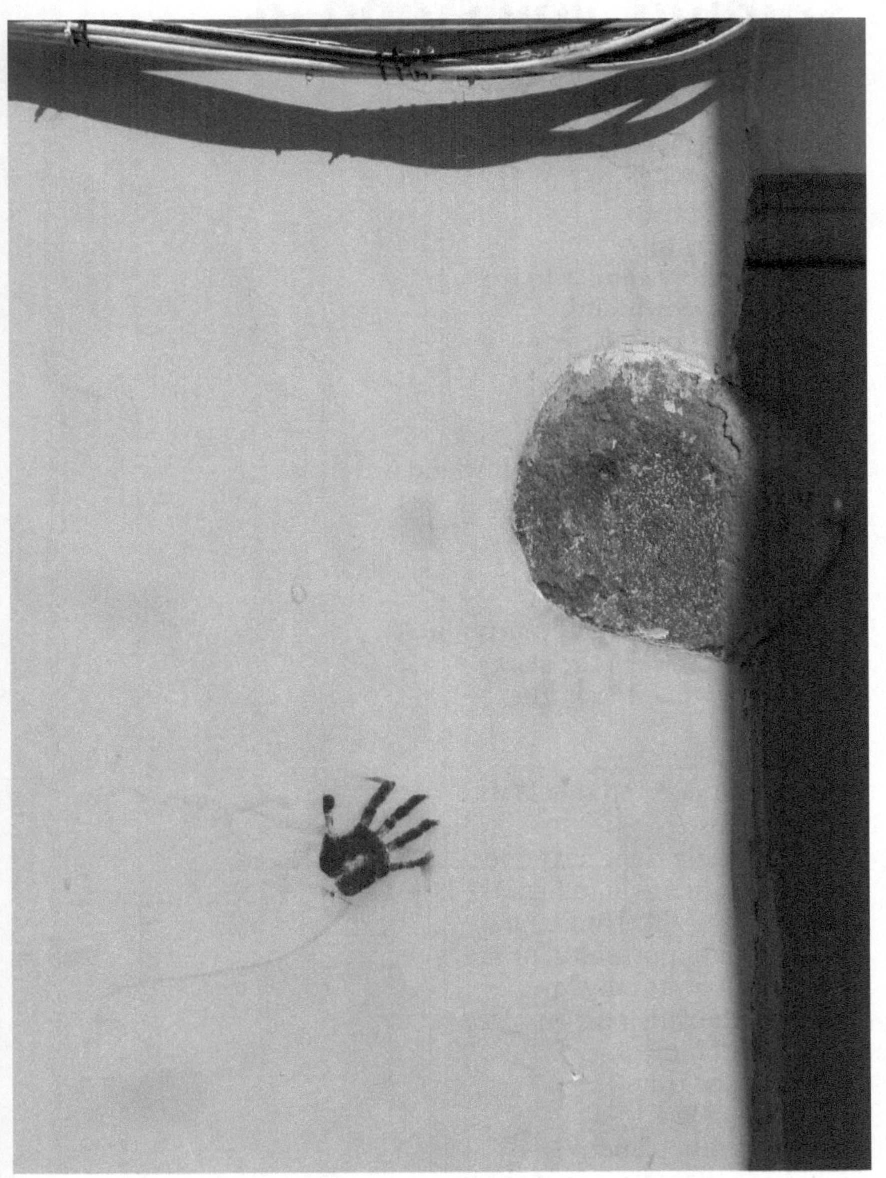

Black Hand, Quito - Roger Camp 85

In a doorway, timid and shining, you stood in silence...

by Marina Kazakova

Clouds seed tears
upon your skin -
probably more similar to frost,
rain pearls slowly sink
deep down the ice layers -
your eyes
are tired metallic mist,
the raindrops are volcanic rocks
like basalt in the Venetian lowlands,
everyone seems to complain
whenever it rains on Earth,
even in Belgium…
Oh, God, lease, rain me
to those shoulders and this umbrella,
let me fall between the stars,
let me see what it feels like
to land
on this flower,
these shoulders, on this Mars.
Mars is close.
It's practically right next door.
It has mountains, and has lake holes,
and recognisable landscapes.
Mars is an opportunity for me
 to carry forward my love,
and yet, the only rain on Mars
is the kind I imagine.
Clouds seed tears
over this
slowly drying planet,
Oh, God, please, rain me there…

Portland Pessimist Society
by Jonathan van Belle

The Portland Pessimist Society was founded in 1984 by Felicia Gay, Rose Brightwell, Gladys Hope, and Joy S. Young. The PPS credo is a four-point "Litany of Grievances":

(1) Gottfried Wilhelm Leibniz is the worst person to have ever lived.

(2) Be disheartened.

(3) Sunshine on the shoulder may lead to skin cancer.

(4) Endism, declinism, kaputism, deathism, and meh-ism are, collectively, high and corollary orthodoxy.

The Caxford Dictionary of 21st-Century Isms:

Meh-ism: *n.* Y'know, whatever; I don't want to argue about it. It is whatever it is.

The following is from an Interview with Cagney Casey, Pulitzer-Prize winning author of Tubby or Not Tubby.

Interviewer: "In *Tubby*, you wrote that 'The contemporary condition is meh-tic, as in the thesis of the meh-ist, a.k.a. meh-ism' Would you care to elaborate?"

CC: "Not really."

A List of Notable Failures

Smith Smith (1907-1973) notable for changing his name to Smith Smith.

Abigail Henderson (1931-1990) notable for eating the most Bonomo's Turkish Taffy in a single sitting.

Larry "Bing Bong" Miller (1940-2010) notable for the most

aggressive promotion of a self-given nickname.

Isabel Lucci (1942-2017) notable for the most suicide attempts in a Dairy Queen (15 attempts; the runner-up: 12 attempts).

A Treatise on the Epistemic Value of Suicide by Arthur Hower

None.

The Mooother Noose Nursery of Versery by Dead Children

There was once an infant, all rosy and warm to the touch;

Now not so much.

IBID.

Interviewer: "Cagney Casey, why do you write?"

CC: "I wrote *Tubby or Not Tubby* in honor of all the victims of optimism, a philosophy that Arthur Hower called 'a bitter mockery of the most unspeakable sufferings of mankind.' I write to undo that bitter mockery."

Interviewer: "You think optimism is a bitter mockery of human suffering?"

CC: "Abel Aganbegyan wrote, and I quote, 'In the Soviet Union we have a saying, a pessimist is someone who believes things can't get any worse. An optimist thinks maybe they can.' Aganbegyan nails it."

Top 5 U.S. Cities In Which to Get a Decent Waffle at 2am

    (1) North Platte, Nebraska

    (2) Scottsbluff, Nebraska

    (3) Ogallala, Nebraska

    (4) McCook, Nebraska

    (5) Falls City, Nebraska

Reclamation

by Vincent A. Alascia

I waited for my dad as I stood in line for food rations under a blue-gray sky streaked by the contrails of war planes. Every Monday for the last eighteen months we had met outside the Klein building for our weekly food vouchers. The combination of drought and the war effort to reclaim Mars had broken the food supply chain. The government stepped in and, well, there we were standing in line to find out if our families would eat this week.

My dad came from the meglev stop down the block. He wasn't moving as fast as the others, but for a man of 97 he was looking surprisingly well. Medical science in the twenty-second century did wonders for our life spans. Too bad everything else was shit. I stepped aside and made room for him. The woman behind me said something nasty but I ignored her. My dad was looking good for his age. He stood about my height, on the tall side of average, with a full head of grey wavy hair. The lines of his face traced frowns as well as smiles. He had his share of both. Most importantly you couldn't see the sickness in him.

The line stretched around the block. "For your country and your health, nutrition is vital," the loudspeakers reminded us every seven minutes. A video marquee displayed an ad for Genrocorp's new Reclamation procedure. "It's much less painful than dying. Molecular disassembly on a whole other order," it said and rattled off all the benefits of the procedure. I shook my head. "That crap should be illegal. Molecular disassembling my ass. It was murder."

Dad looked up at me. "People like to think they have a choice. You can't begrudge 'em that."

"That's no choice."

"The courts would disagree. Beside it's been centuries since assisted suicide became legal. This is nothing more than the evolution of that. Plus, there's some benefits."

"So they claim. Besides, since when did you become such a fan?"

Before my dad could answer, the peace officer waved us on. We entered the building and quickly picked up our vouchers. As usual we spent one of them on lunch in the attached diner.

The room's design was that of an old twentieth century railroad car dinner, complete with red vinyl seats, Formica tables, and even black and white checkered floor. We slid into a booth next to the door and ordered the usual, eggs, meat, and some fruit. Our coffee came quickly, and I settled back, glad to be off my feet for once.

Dad took a sip of his coffee and looked over the cup at me. "You know I decided to sign myself up for Reclamation."

The coffee mug in my hand trembled. "What? When did you decide that? The treatments have been going so well."

Dad shook his head. "It's not that, well it is. I just know that this is the end for me, I've faced it and I settled my mind on that, now I think I want to do something more."

I slam my coffee cup down, eliciting some startled glances in our direction. "Something more? And you think striping out every last bit of material from your body is something more?"

"If it improves someone else's life, I do." Dad's eyes took on a distant look. He wasn't listening to me anymore, but that only made me angrier.

I lowered my voice. "The point is you've been given a second chance." The robotic server floated by our table and shot some more coffee into our cups from the nozzle on the end of one of the eight appendages protruding from its round squat metal body. "You just want to throw all that away?"

He shook his head and smiled at me. "No. Son, you have to realize, I have Reinfeld's Cobalt disease. There is no cure. My body will literally eat itself up if I don't go insane first."

"You've been doing good." My eyes pleaded with him. "The treatments are working. Another six months you could be in full remission."

Dad shoved some eggs in his mouth and shrugged. "Yeah or the symbionts they inject to keep the disease in check could collect in my brain. I could wind up a drooling idiot with one large parasite where my brain used to be." Dad took a sip from his coffee. The corner of his right eye twitched so minutely that only someone close to him with knowledge of his illness would catch it. "Look, I know we don't live forever, I've been closer than ever to that realization. The last thing I want is to just be some pile of decomposing organic matter. I want my death to be an opening for someone else."

I looked down at my tin plate with the perfectly proportioned amount of eggs, hash browns and some kind of orange gel. I didn't feel like eating any more.

"Then donate your body to science *after* you die. You know once you sign up for reclamation, they take you. What about the rest of us? Jenny and the kids? We're still alive and want you in our lives."

He shook his head. "It's not like that. In the contract I specify the date and even time of my disassembly. I figure before that we can all have one last weekend together at the coast, you and Sara, Jenny and the kids. We'll make it a real family vacation."

I couldn't hide my anger anymore. "Oh, sure the vacation just before Grandpa goes off to die." I waited for him to say something, but instead he just kept it to himself. "You know if mom was still alive…"

"I wouldn't be doing this if your mother was still around."

"Damn it!" I slammed my hand on the table. The officer at the door looked our way. His hand moved to his rifle. I smiled at him and lowered my voice to a sharp whisper. "Damn it,

Dad, you're saying the rest of us don't matter?"

He laid his fork down and sighed. "No, that's not it either. I don't want to be a burden. Your mother at least had me, you never had to see how bad she got, what this disease did to her. I'm not about to inflict that on you or your sister. The mornings I had to wake up and find her ice cold and shaking. The screaming and cries for the pain to just go away. You weren't there for all of that." Dad's eyes grew dark with the memories.

I leaned back away from the table. Our time was up and there were plenty of other hungry people outside waiting for our seats. "I'm not going to change your mind on this one."

"It means the world to me how much you're trying, but no. I've made my decision. Actually, I already filled out all the paperwork."

I shook my head. "Of course, you did."

Once we were outside, I hugged him. I thought about asking how much time he had. Would I see him again? What weekend should I clear? I watched him walk up the block to the underground maglev. I couldn't let go of the idea that I was watching him walk away from me forever.

Back at work my mind couldn't focus on much of anything. It didn't help matters that we were several days behind on processing a shipment of ore from the asteroid belt mining operation. Trains of cars stacked the rail lines into and out of the plant. They moved like sulking beasts clanging together in an ominous drone that drowned out the roaring of the furnace fires. The engineers got to sit up in the control room and push all the buttons, but the mechanics like myself were stuck down here, greasy and sweating among the lumbering boxes of steel and stone. We wondered how long before the next clank of the cars would be the last and our shifts ended. Now was not the time to let my mind wander. I guess what happened next was inevitable.

I came to on a gurney. Bodies moved quickly around me. Gowns, gloves, and masks. I tried to move my head for a better look but couldn't. A stasis field held me in place.

"Blood pressure is steady now, heart rate and oxygen levels improving."

"He took a whole cart of ore to the legs. Where are they?"

"Not enough left to scrape off."

It was then that I realized I had no feeling below my stomach. Where were my legs? I tried to jerk my body up. I tried to scream at the people. What happened to my fucking legs!

"He's coming to, better increase the meds."

The sensation was of a cloud washing over me. The light shifted from stark white to a blueish tint. Warmth crept up my arms and over my torso. It felt like a huge blanket lay over me. I blinked my eyes and when they opened, the trauma center was gone. I stood on a grassy field. I could see the ocean beyond it. The memories rushed over my mind. Summer 2057. That week on the coast of Maryland. I could smell the salt in the air and feel the ocean breeze tickling the hairs around my ears. The sky was blue, a shade I hadn't seen in a long time. I looked around, and I knew my dad and mother wouldn't be far. We were just coming back from buying the food for the week. My older brother and I rushed out of the car as our mother worked on freeing my sister from her car seat as my dad yelled at us to get back and help with the bags. I was about to turn when I realized I was all alone. The picture was fading, not the memory just the perception of it right now.

The pungent smell of antiseptic gel burst through my nasal passages. I blinked my eyes open and saw my wife sitting in the chair across from me. Sunlight peeked through the closed gray curtains. I drew in a deep breath and let it out just as quickly. My wife looked up and came to my side.

"Don't try to move."

It was then that I realized I ached all over. If pain were a shroud of fuzzy pin pricks and barbed wire, I wore it from head to toe. Just then I felt the sheets pressing against a big toe. Feet. I had feet and legs, two of them. Was it all a dream? I tried to move again but nothing happened. The strain on my face as my head rose from the pillow caught my wife's eye.

"You can't move." She placed a hand on my chest. "You've been under so long that your muscles have atrophied. You won't be able to move them just yet."

"How long have I been here?" I settled back on the pillow, blinking.

She hesitated, biting down on her lower lip. "Five weeks. The coma was induced to help your body accept…"

I knew what she was going to say. "My legs." I looked around the room. "Where's my Dad? He had put in for reclamation. That's the last thing I remember before returning to work. "These legs, tell me they aren't his."

She shook her head. "They wanted to clone legs for you, but there wasn't enough material left of your original ones and stem cells would have taken too long to grow into new ones. Your Dad moved up his reclamation. The molecular blueprint he provided was enough to get you the cloned legs."

I closed my eyes and turned away. I didn't want to hear any more. I'd become the thing I wanted least. The reason for my dad to go ahead with this damn procedure. I might have been able to live with the idea of some stranger getting a second chance but for that person to be me. For it to be me lying in that bed knowing that my dad is no longer on this Earth because of me. I know it was foolish and instead I should cherish the part of him that is now part of me. I'm too angry for that now. Maybe one day, my view will change, but not now. I miss my dad, legs, or no legs, I still miss my dad.

how i came
(after eve ewing)

by ellie sharp

1.
in the pistachio-shell hours of some thousand grassy nights.
innumerable like feet on street corners
and all their destinations.

my mom's new car belonged to someone's old son,
its duct-tape flapping as she speeds, the bumper banging along,
happily and in disruption, mile after mile afterrrr

2.
i walked from one city to the next and found them the same.
a rusty gate groans its lonesome and is kept closed
but never shut. i look at the face of something silent and viscous
and see only interruption.

3.
i came from a snail's shell

from its goo too.

4.
and there are you
like a moth intrudes on light, like light.

and here is me
and we in the ways hips flutter like wings
or other things that don't know what to do with themselves.

5.
like a flooded bathtub. towel up against the door.
left there long after.

Whither the Wheel

by AJD*

We endure. We get by.
We wither and die.

The ends draw us in.
The river stays dry.

The plains sing a song
of bitter lament.

The mountains think better
and will not repent.

Seasons turn, climates change.
We cry from the wheel, in vain, remain.

We endure. We get by.
We wither, and then, we die.

Youth shout foul, from rampart, from dike.
We need not sleepwalk through death's early gate.

Change now, while we can, a sensible demand.
Don't you see? Won't you try? Are you dumb?

The programming is bad, but better over here.
Share power, tax wealth, leave oil underground.

Adapt, evolve. Live by the codes you proclaim.
Act like there's a tomorrow you won't cheat or fear.

With such sentiment, ardent appeals fire into cloud.
The braindead megaphone unwinds, yet dominates.

From alley, from wood, brave youth reemerge,
unfazed by big lies, speaking truth to your tower.

You brought hell to our earth, became your fake devil.
You took without looking. Now denial's ascendant.

Your damaging extractions, artful justifications,
the fatal convenience of things as they are...

It's true, we know. We see. It's there. It's here.
We call you out, us as well.

Patting heads, walking away, your eyes stay averted.
Proud and oblivious, you double down on the blight.

Blind bots gaslight to echo chamber: Sell, baby, buy!
Don't dare miss out. Last drops of dream, on sale tonight.

Revolution foiled, mopping Wall Street's tight brow,
everything's your wake, a steamroller of greed.

Alternatives drowned in a pool of bent light,
neoliberalism's stalking horse reaps ill-gotten heed.

Yet you glance with concern to empire's periphery,
when the threat grows inside, no ending this history.

We endure. Some get by. A few better than others.
  For now, for now.

The ends will come. And we all wither, and die.
  Of course, of course.

But the wheel has a way, of turning around.

Shaking heads, youth demur. That's not what we meant.
No to more war, the turn into carnage, barbaric descent.

We can choose an enlightened path, it's clear, please see.
Defenders of privilege can step aside without combat.

There is still time to crush the insidious hand,
bring the walls down, open guarded vaults to all.

Then we'll live like we should, cherishing the world,
as it turns us out, and in, through life and death.

We'll plan for seven generations, grow with good faith,
in peace, in balance. No market for pain.

Together with science, with love and understanding,
we'll accept all the turnings of nature's great rings.

But first we'll disembark your one-way killing train.

We endure, we get by.
We sprout up to the sky.

The wheel rolls over.
Birds flutter and fly.

Tracks fill in,
water of life.

Bacteria swim free,
and games start again.

---

*In November 2019, when covid was a baby, a customer in the city of books
approached the cashiers during a lull at the start of an author event. Bemused
by our inactivity, the person (possibly named Frank Pool) inquired as to our
condition. I replied, "We endure. We get by." M. Pool responded, "We wither
and die." AJD completed this polemic in difficult doggerel based on that and
wished to acknowledge the assistance.

Limestone and Rose Quartz
by Jesse Sensibar

Sometimes you walk in darkness, sometimes you walk in light. You get betrayed in ways large and small, at the same time you get lifted up in ways large and small. Sometimes the hand that reaches out to you is something large to grab onto that holds you firmly in its grip, sometimes it's the tiny finger of a child but still I smile and rise every morning like looking into the setting sun behind your blonde perm on a concrete and brick stoop on Blackstone Avenue in the spring of 1985.

Waiting for Dogot
by L. Fid

"Yes. Did you hear it again?"

"Shit, if it's what I think it is, well. Shit's gonna 'splode. In a good way."

"What's that? What is going to explode? Let me tell you oh sleepy one "

"Yes, you heard! Me too. Do you think? Do you think it is?"

"Wait, no, nothing."

Apropos nothing, the cat, whose ear twitches I'd been lazily engaging in dialogue with for several minutes, jumped off my stomach and onto the concrete floor.

She walked gingerly towards the center of the room, eyes fixed at a point under the stairs, tail swishing slightly. She crouched, positioning as if to pounce. She held still for thirty seconds before relaxing. Gradually, she tilted onto her side and fell asleep.

With an awful grunt, I propped myself into less of a recline on the thin futon. I adjusted my line of sight across the cluttered coffee table to keep track of her ear ticks -- our key to survival, I was sure.

"Yes. We keen them together."

She lifted her head from atop her forepaws, shook it, then lowered it back down.

"No? You don't accept my 'them'? An epistemological question?"

She turned and opened her eyes slightly, then went back to sleep.

"Anyway. You know who we're waiting for."

The ears stayed still for almost two minutes.

After mustering my strength, I staggered over, picked her up, and brought her back. I held her over the table as I lay down on my side, then placed her on my hip. She entered into a fugue state which I knew to usually precede a deep sleep.

Since I needed her ears, I continued our dialogue. "I suppose it could be anyone, in a way. Many might serve the purpose. But you know who is likely coming."

The cat's ears pulled back into an acute angle, then twitched three times, before slowly ending in their resting position.

"Okay, all those under the nomenclature 'them' are of course a subset of the 'universal one,' which we discussed previously."

The cat shifted, farted.

"Exactly. The fart and the farter. But "

The cat jerked upward, then slowly rotated her neck and head as her reclining body stayed still. She paused at an orientation towards the top of the stairs. I leaned in to make sure. Her eyes were still closed.

"What?" I whispered. Nothing.

She stayed in position, seemingly unconscious or entranced. Eventually, she yawned, returned her head to her paws and entered into deep sleep. I shook my head.

"You've been doing that routine all night. What do you mean? Who has your ear?"

I leaned back onto the rickety couch at her non-response. Not just the basement, but the entire complex seemed preternaturally still. I listened to nothing intensely for a long time. I remembered a street fair I'd attended as a child -- all the cacophony, whirl and rumble -- and then, home, blackout and sheet forts in the basement. All the buzz gone, just earth.

It's still here, though. The buzz, the hum. I reached out with my body, felt as much as heard the reassuring electronic purrs. My mind's eye elsewhere, a voice chimed out from a cardboard box atop the coffee table, beneath a pile of old clothes.

"What do you see now?" and "Can you tell who is on which side?" then "Oh, please be careful." All muffled, but discernible.

I seemed to be hearing one side of a conversation. The box contained a variety of recently discarded electronic devices, including a wideband receiver which must have still held some battery charge. I surmised that I could be listening to a ham radio channel, pulled in from waves of ether which nearly circumnavigate the globe at night.

In a flash, I felt uncertain, wondering if some cell phone had accidentally been thrown in the mix. The words might be arriving through local towers and geosynchronous satellites.

Did I recognize the voice? It was too weak to tell. The half conversation faded away. The cat stayed asleep.

I thought about going in the other room, to bed, so comfortable. I thought about getting up, investigating the broadcast or call, making food or doing dishes, taking a stab at all the things. I stayed still and looked at the cat's ears.

I woke up with the cat's paws on my neck, kneading flesh but withholding her claws. Disoriented, I did not immediately realize I had been asleep. The room tilted and spun in vertigo before I dropped into free fall. I clutched the front edge of the couch for support. The cat put a paw on my cheek.

"Yes? Is it time?" I looked towards the stairs. The cat extended her sharp nails into my face. "Ow." I pushed her back onto my lap and sat up. She curled into a ball and turned her head upside down. She blinked her eyes and continued staring at me.

"I see. The 'time' concept again. Time is moving forward because space is expanding. Gravity warps it. If we were to build a time machine and go back a day, we'd need to travel tens of thousands of miles through space, and we'd need a supercomputer to calculate where this room is for a moment, a moment we need to slice as finely as possible. Then we'd need to find a way to match the spinning velocity of the earth so the transition would not be so violent and "

The cat twisted and rolled onto the ruffled blanket next to me. She arched her back and turned away.

"No, of course we won't. Why bother? All timelines converge and here we are."

She curled up again, her face towards the back of the couch this time. Her shallow breathing slowed and she was practically immobile.

"Don't you hear them anymore? Your ears have been so still."

As if on cue, her left ear twitched twice, her right once. Then, a pounding of feet down the stairs next door. We both winced, turned inward. Not for us.

After some period of silence, we went on. Three more twitches.

"Yes, yes. Yes. The trinity. The magical, transcendent third which creates the world, beyond abstractions. Transcending polarities, energy is converted to matter and here we come. The many from three. Everything. Over time, you "

She twitched twice, first one ear, then the other.

"Oh, you. 'You.' The concept." I shifted into an attitude of responsive repose, contorting my body around hers and continued in a softer tone. "Well, the second, uh, 'person,' as you will, is of course the first separation. Some say 'I.' I say 'you.' The two in you is the superimposition of a division of the world into a so-called knowledge system based on opposites."

She pulled both ears back at once and released them slowly. I turned to look over my back and shoulder to the stairs, then to the other room, the cabinet drawers, the small high window, the painted over door, before returning my attention to her.

"Black, white. Hot, cold. Good, evil. By dividing, separating into twos, we can apprehend it, ingest it, consume it. The world, that is. We create our imaginariums there, in first division. All of our mental constructs start here."

I scratched my belly, then hers. She stretched out a paw and pushed herself away from the back of the couch.

"Of course, there are no opposites in the manifestation. There's no opposite to a rock or a tree. We forget, lose sight of the arbitrary origin of our situation. With the context lost, an attachment to symbols inevitably sets in."

She covered her eyes with a paw.

"'Two' is also just a point in 'one-two-three.'" I rubbed her belly again.

She wrapped my hand, held it in place with forepaw claws, kicked me with her hind legs. "Ah, ah, ah. Let me just "

I used my other arm to disengage and separate us, though not without some bloody punctures and scratches.

"All this duality has nothing to do with 'you,' of course," I said, sitting erect again. "You are wonderful and awful both. We're part of everything, always. And nothing, if we can find it, outside our idea of it. I'm not sure if nothing is an abstraction or not."

The cat took a swipe at my arm, still dripping blood, coming close but missing. She pulled her arm beneath her body, eyes glowing.

"You're me and we're all. One. It all comes back to "

The voice returned. Rather, a different voice from the same box. The other side of the conversation, possibly. Muffled from beneath the pile of abandoned apparel.

"I can see them turning away now. They're going in the other direction. I think they won't be back. We'll see." After a pause, "We'll be left alone tonight, I'd say."

The cat turned to look towards the sound, then the stairs, before curling up in the folds of the blanket to sleep. The voice faded away again.

I thought I heard something on the top landing. I could not see the cat's ears, concealed as she was in the blanket, and felt at a loss. I considered rising to find out what I could. Instead, I leaned back into the couch and closed my eyes. The cat started snoring softly.

New Arrival

by Mickey Collins

Was that my door I heard? I slowly rose and crawled to my door. Who was this new arrival at my door? I wasn't expecting guests. Surely if any friends were going to stop by they would have phoned ahead. Did I pay the phone bill?

If I press my ear against the door, perhaps I could hear who was on the other side. I wait, but don't hear anything. My door is too thick. The locks, too many.

I move myself under the window, surreptitiously. It takes me an entire minute to raise my hand to the curtain, and another to slowly pull it aside. So slow that any movement seen from outside would be imperceptible. I hope.

When I was younger I lived in a house with windows on all sides. From the living room you could see the front door and they could see you. There was no hope for you if someone wanted to sell you something, like religion or cookies. There was no pretending you weren't in.

From my vantage point I can just barely see the blue sky that is beyond my front door. The view is uninterrupted. Meaning no one is at the door. Or maybe the person is too short for me to see?

I slide my back down the wall after easing the curtain closed again. Back at the door, I raise up until I'm just to the left of the peephole. If I move my eye quickly enough past it, I may be able to see outside and peer down at my uninvited, short-of-stature intruder without them seeing how the light changes through it. I hold my breath and jerk my neck to the right. Nothing. It was a blur. If I were to try again, I would risk alerting them to my presence.

I curse myself that it has come to this. I gently grab hold of the top-most lock with my thumb and index finger. I push into the door to soften the lock's turning. Once complete, I move onto the chain lock and glide it without pushing or pulling too hard. I'm reminded to get more WD-40. Finally comes the deadbolt, a point of no return. Once it is unlocked there is nothing between my safety and the outside world. I push and turn it, the door creaks slightly, but it's all over now. If my guest had walked away, surely they would be turning back now hearing the door open. My heart races as the sun's rays fill the room from the growing gap I've created.

I shade my eyes with a hand to mitigate the harsh light. I prepare myself for a sudden retreat back inside. I look left, right, up and then down.

No one. On the porch sits a cardboard box. I bend down and slide the box inside, keeping an eye out for any dangers as I do. I shut the door quickly, but quietly, relock one, two, three and set to work opening the box.

It's the security camera I ordered. And just in time too. I couldn't imagine another package like this one just sitting out there for anyone to take. There are too many strangers in the world.

108 *Untitled - Jeremy Szuder*

守株待兔
Like Waiting for a Rabbit in Your Lap

Adaptation by Sue Su
Translation by Robert Eversmann

很久很久以前，有一个农民，每天都很辛苦地工作。有一天，他正在休息，突然，有一只兔子，一下子撞到了他旁边的树根上，死了。

那一天，他吃了很美味的晚饭。

可是从那以后，他不工作了，每天守在树根旁边，希望有其他的兔子撞死在树根上，这样他就又可以吃到很美味的饭了！

There was once there was a farmer who worked hard everyday. But one day he decided to rest and so sat beneath a tree. Suddenly, a rabbit rushed beside him, tripped and broke its neck.

That day the farmer feasted.

The farmer never worked again, but instead remained beneath the tree, wishing it might gift a second rabbit.

note: *This story is based on the four-character phrase,* 守株待兔 (shǒu zhū dài tù). *Four-character phrases, like English idioms, are used in everyday speech.* 守株待兔 *is used to describe someone who falls into luck for nothing.*

滥竽充数
Will the Real Pan-Piper, Please Stand Up?

Adaptation by Sue Su

Translation by Robert Eversmann

很久很久以前，齐国的皇帝爱听吹竽，又非常喜欢热闹，所以为他吹竽的就有三百人。他常常叫这三百人一起吹竽给他听。有个南郭先生，完全不会吹竽，但是因为吹竽的人很多，所以他假装和别人一样会吹竽。

后来这位老皇帝死了，新皇帝喜欢听人一个一个地吹竽。南郭先生听到这个，非常害怕，只好逃走，不再假装自己很会吹竽了。

An emperor in the time of Warring states loved listening to panpipes. The emperor loved panpipes best of all intensely loud. And so he rustled up three-hundred pipers, a band he ordered, Pipe! But in this band there was a certain Mr. Bo—a Mr. Bo who could not pipe. However, in a crowd so large, who notices the one bad piper in a chorus of three-hundred?

But as is the way with generations, out with the old emperor, in with the new. This new emperor however did not at all like loudness and ordered the band disband. Instead he lined the pipers up and each one ordered, Pipe! But there was a certain Mr. Bo—a Mr. Bo who could not pipe. However, when it came his turn to solo, he ran from the castle and fled for his life.

note: This story is based on the four-character phrase, 滥竽充数 *(làn yú chōng shù). Four-character phrases, like English idioms, are used in everyday speech.* 滥竽充数 *is used to mean that it's easy to get by pretending in a chorus, but if you're asked to solo you better run.*

What Are You Good At?
by Scott Laudati

I don't remember when it started
but the end came last Tuesday.
I'd taken a Xanax and slept all day,
seeing an old girlfriend
and my dead dog
in dreams or nightmares
or some other hell that I'll get to relive
if I don't get this one right.
And when I finally woke
I couldn't ignore what all the bad poems
and awful music had been telling me:
I'd lived too long,
there aren't going to be new chapters in my book,
there won't be any more songs.
This can happen to some at ninety
and others at thirty.
But I think for most it never happens
and that's why rational people still breed
without any fear
of consequence.
Don't they see the holes in everything?
Don't they know there's no second coming?
Most people start dying from the minute
they're born. It
took me thirty-five years to give up
and sometimes
I'm still proud of that.
The world didn't want a new poet,
but there's always room for another plumber.

Congratulations, It's a Boy
by J. Ian Bush

By age five, his father was doing his best to make a man of him.
He had unusual methods:

1) Burrowing both fists into the shoulder blades, elbows deep
(this will teach him how to eat pain).

2) Sculpting his silhouette to fit some kind of monster.

3) Transfiguring his hands into shovels by applying some
strange alchemy making him dig a hole from the belly through
the chest cavity, carving out enough room for a punching bag.

4) Trapping the voice box in his fist like a lighting bug, tighten-
ing his grip until there's no more space for its glow.

Weeping Willow
by Anum Sattar

is it shame of making love
to a low ranking general
that your fingers tremble
while undoing my sash?

silly foot soldier
I would scream in delight
being taken from behind
were your overweight wife
not peeping through the blinds!

It was common in the Edo period for Oirans or Japanese courtesans to have professional names inspired by scenes from nature: "young willow," "budding willow," "bright rock," "spring rain," "morning chrysanthemum," etc.

The shogun affectionately called his mistress a "weeping willow" mistakenly believing that she was uncomfortable in his presence.

Lightning Bugs in a Mason Jar, Summer of 1998, Moments Before a Disaster

by J. Ian Bush

It's the summer of 1998. I'm given a mason jar. Almost everything is black. My father hasn't made me bleed yet. He jokes that the grass is high enough to disappear in. He smells like Budweiser but his eyes don't reek of violence. There are lightning bugs. He grabs one. Smashes it. Makes his open palm glow. He tells me that even when their hearts stop beating the blood is still beautiful. Instead I decide to capture some. To keep them in one solid piece. It's the summer of 1998. I'm learning that making something bleed can never be beautiful. I still don't want to disappear. It's the summer of 1998. There is my father. He smells like Budweiser but hasn't made me bleed yet.

The Box
by John Chrostek

You are living in a box
Growing smaller. You were born inside the box,
and it has been a part of you (apart from you)
forever, like a shadow is and isn't, like the walls
the shadows play on or the fires that cast them.
A shadow is its light. In such a manner, so's the
box.

You can fit the universe inside the box, a dio-
rama of the sacred Things that make your
box your own and no one else's, or so they
say. Anything can be inside the box: the moon,
its gentle hand, ripe geraniums in spring, even
the rare sight of a hundred people who all
somehow still like each other running in a field
just by the river. Everything can fit inside the
box, all volume a finite limit spread out to the
boundary walls of the box. Just never further.

The walls are closing in a little every day. Your
apartment was never so tiny, your scooter was
a van or a station wagon, it was the Mystery
Machine, it fit like twenty in the back, but the
box is definitely shrinking and now there is no
room for mystery.

What it is that you remember and what it is that
you still got has all got to fit inside the box.

You want to cry about the box, try to cut out all
the clutter so what matters inside pops, but there's
no popping out the box. There'll never be a
window or a door that'll take you out the box.

You could be an angry little man about the box.
You could build a big ol' drill inside the box,

make it the sharpest, hardest thing that's ever
been inside the box, the great almighty Babel
Phallus designed by the minds of heaven
to break us free of the box, but if there was
something tough enough to get
outside the box, that isn't the wall.
That isn't the box.
You used to have a yard inside
the box, but the yard has been
condensed a little, and outer
space is waiting for you, just
at the end of the street.

You're wearing a little
spacesuit in the box (sweet),
but also a wide-brimmed
sun hat, on account of
how much you love
summer.

Summer used to be so
great inside the box.
You can see a world,
looking outwards,
that might could be
beyond the box.

It's the spot someone
would be standing to
get a look inside the box,
and say aloud "Oh, look
at that, that's lovely."
But you've never seen
somebody there.
You wish so often you
did.

So you look to what
surrounds you in your
little box, that which
casts a light or moves
like shadow, the people
stuck inside it all with

you, the little bits of dream
you save every day the box
gets smaller,
to keep your soul
in motion, the colors,
lights and sounds collaged
beside you that let you
Know this box has been
your home,

that you are all your memories
and your joys, that this box of
yours has not been yours alone
to die inside.

If there's really nothing
else outside the box,
those memories
and people are
everything.
They're as you
as you will
ever get

to be.

Apocalypso Lemonade
by Jonathan van Belle

I once dreamt that I was gunned down. My hands, poor shields, tore open without a sound. My right cheek and right row of teeth were shattered, sprayed off. I could only crawl, and crawling, only feebly hide from my exterminator. The exterminator walked up, took his time, aimed, and shot calmly—over and over. At last, only my arm offered the motility to slug along the ground; I bled along the ground as I crawled. The chewed rags of my cheek swept along too. I saw from a worm's height. I lifted the shreds of my left hand to block the final bullet. Again, my exterminator took his time, walked very close, aimed at my face—to smear it out—and, without hesitation, perhaps without much interest, my exterminator fired his gun.

Now here is a recipe for the end of days:

Apocalypso Lemonade

Ingredients:

1 species of lemon tree, burnt
1 shot of sperm
2 reproductively active humans
3 cups of glacier, melted

Directions:

In a blender, combine lemon tree, sperm, humans, and melted glacier.
Blend until smooth.
Pour into the ocean.

But what is a cocktail without some mood music? But what is the proper instrument for one's last bit of music and cocktail? For me, it would be the piano, scintillating piano.

Under the tinkle of a piano, a person could happily slow dance with their exterminator. But what song? That is simple to answer: I composed my own song (without melody) for piano:

Piano Man, where's your head?
Why all this red?
$15 piano wire and a bridge,
And a leap,
A choking slice and clean,
Quick, and cheap.

there are too many poems about morning

by ellie sharp

i wake in the belly of a fasting beast
a broken day devouring itself.
there are too many poems about morning
i announce

to my empty room. a loose bouquet
of light drifts to where you last lay
still
the shadow of your leaving

scrawled against the wall.
there is no night left in this bed.
once
drunk off the stars i dreamed

the moon had your face. day came
with the same inevitability of heartbreak
as it always comes
the sky tied together with solitude.

lately, time has revealed itself
as a mirror.
i watch your hands unbutton a map
and flatten it across your knees.

have you ever touched a mountaintop?
you whisper. has the sky ever reached downwards
and swept you up? have you ever been touched
here or here and like this?

do you like this?
the clock on my wall sighs a sigh
that resists finish. come, it seems to say,
stain these sheets with your touch.

Bios

GALE ACUFF

I have had poetry published in *Ascent, Chiron Review, Pennsylvania Literary Journal, Poem, Adirondack Review, Maryland Poetry Review, Florida Review, Slant, Nebo, Arkansas Review, South Dakota Review*, and many other journals. I have authored three books of poetry, all from BrickHouse Press: *Buffalo Nickel, The Weight of the World*, and *The Story of My Lives*. I have taught university English courses in the US, China, and Palestine.

AJD

AJD was once a bookseller.

VINCENT A. ALASCIA

Vincent A. Alascia is the author of, "The Hole In Your Mind," "Undead Heart," "In the Presence of Gods," and, "Xristos: Chosen of God," available on Kindle and paperback as well as works that have appeared in anthologies and online. Originally an East Coast native, he makes his home in the Portland Oregon area with his wife. Vincent has been a librarian for over 15 years and is also a musician. He is currently working on a Steampunk Horror novel and a guide to reading Tarot.

KUMMAM AL-MAADEED

Kummam Al-Maadeed is an author from Qatar, who believes in magic and the existence of fairy worlds. She started writing in 2007 when she was attending Qatar University to study Mass Communications. She now works at Qatar University as a Section Head of Media & Publications, as she dreams about her next novel. *The Lost Rose* is her debut best-selling novel.

MAEV BARBA

Dr. Maev Barba attended the Puget Sound Writer's Conference in 2018. She is a PNW native and a great lover of books. She used to sell books door-to-door. A doctor of astronomy, Barba looks into space and considers neither the small as too little, nor the large as too great, for the lover of stars knows there is no limit to dimension.

LILY BRADFIELD

Lily Bradfield loves writing both short fiction and non-fiction—she has been previously published in both the online and print editions of *Cultured Magazine*, an art and design periodical, as well as Vassar College's literary magazine.

J. Ian Bush

J. Ian Bush is an Ohioan poet who is interested in the confessional and surreal. Their first chapbook, "Route 23 to Golgotha" was published by EMP books, a small press, in early 2019. Ever since, they have been selling copies online, as well as at live readings. They also run a house venue in their city, where a regular poetry reading is held, as well as other local performing artists. Their work has been featured in various magazines and journals.

Roger Camp

Roger Camp is the author of three photography books including the award-winning *Butterflies in Flight* (Thames & Hudson, 2002) and *Heat* (Charta, Milano, 2008). His work has appeared in numerous journals including *The New England Review*, *New York Quarterly*, and the *Vassar Review*. He previously worked as a reference librarian at the Santa Ana Public Library and as an analytical bibliographer for the director of the Humanities Research Center at the University of Texas, Austin.

John Chrostek

John Chrostek is a Pushcart-nominated poet, playwright and author who works at Powell's City of Books in Portland, OR. His work has been featured in publications such as *Artemis*, *River Heron Review*, and *Cathexis Press*.

Mickey Collins

~~Mickey rights wrongs. Mickey wrongs rites.~~ Mickey writes words, sometimes wrong words but he tries to get it write.

Sunset Combs

Sunset Combs is a recent Earlham College graduate who is heading to Colorado State University in the fall to earn her Master's in Creative Nonfiction.

Robert Eversmann

Robert Eversmann works for Deep Overstock. His website is roberteversmann.com

L. Fid

L. Fid is a member of a pseudonymous arts collective dedicated to world domination.

Phoebe Glen

Phoebe Glen is a writer who self-published *Sexcapades: Lessons in Sex Ed* in 2017. Originally from Arizona, she landed in Portland, Oregon, after living abroad in Europe for three years. She enjoys sharing stories and her opinions with everyone, and is passionate about creating a more comprehensive Sex Education in the USA. Find more of her writing at http://phoebeglen.com/

Dianah Hughley

Dianah Hughley has been a bookseller for Powell's Books since 2008. She mainly writes staff pick reviews, so this essay is a big stretch for her. She works in the blue room and specializes in literary and Pacific Northwest fiction. She lives in Portland with her husband and many, many -- too many -- books.

Matthew Hunt

Matthew Hunt is a burgeoning poet, outdoorsman, and a traveler of the world. He was born and raised in southern Georgia. Matt worked for years in a bookstore surrounded by the comfort of the written word. He currently lives in Washington, DC with his wife and children.

Erin Karbuczky

Erin Karbuczky is a Lead Bookseller at Powell's Books, and an avid reader and book collector. Her mission as a bookseller is to unite each person with the perfect book for them, so that they may grow to love reading as much as she does. She resides in the Pacific Northwest with her husband, their cat, and a head full of stories aching to share with the world.

Marina Kazakova

Marina Kazakova is a Russian-born Belgium-based poet-performer, currently working on the practice-based PhD in Arts "Lyric Poem: A research on how the unique characteristics of lyric poetry can be expressed in audio-visual medium" at KULeuven/LUCA School of arts.

Melissa Kerman

My name is Melissa Kerman and I'm a writer from Long Island.

Ariel Kusby

Ariel Kusby is a writer and bookseller based in Portland, Oregon. She currently works in the Rose and Orange rooms at Powell's City of Books, where she pays special attention to children's books about witches, odd cookbooks, and gnome gardening guides. You can check out her writing at www.arielkusby.com.

Scott Laudati
Scott Laudati's recent work has appeared in *The Cardiff Review* and *The Columbia Journal*. He spends most of his time with a 14 year-old schnoodle named Dolly. Visit him on social media @ScottLaudati.

Faith Noelle
I am a 24-year old writer of both contemporary and fantasy fiction, currently living in Pennsylvania while I pursue a doctoral degree in clinical psychology. I have had work previously published in the University of Richmond's *The Messenger*. I have also previously worked as an editor for *VERSE* literary journal.

Timothy Arliss O'Brien
Timothy Arliss O'Brien is an interdisciplinary artist in music composition, writing, and visual arts. His goal is to connect people to accessible new music that showcases virtuosic abilities without losing touch of authentic emotions. He has premiered music with The Astoria Music Festival, Cascadia Composers, Sound of Late's 48 hour Composition Competition and ENAensemble's Serial Opera Project. He also wants to produce writing that connects the reader to themselves in a way that promotes wonder and self realization. He has published several novels (*Dear God I'm a Faggot*, *They*), and has written for Look Up Records (Seattle), Our Bible App, and *Deep Overstock: The Bookseller's Journal*. He has also combined his passion for poetry with his love of publishing and curates the podcast The Poet Heroic. He also showcases his makeup skills as the phenomenal drag queen Tabitha Acidz.
Check out more of his writing, and his full discography at his website: www.timothyarlissobrien.com

Michael Santiago
Michael Santiago is a serial expat, avid traveler, and writer of all kinds. Originally from New York City, and later relocating to Rome in 2016 and Nanjing in 2018. He enjoys the finer things in life like walks on the beach, existential conversations and swapping murder mystery ideas. Keen on exploring themes of humanity within a fictitious context and aspiring author.

Anum Sattar
Anum Sattar is a recent graduate from College of Wooster in Ohio, USA. She won the first Grace Prize and third Vonna Hicks poetry awards at the college.
Her poems have been published in the *American Journal of Poetry* (Margie), *Under the Basho, Indicia*: a journal curating literary arts, *Calliope* by Writers'

Special Interest Group (SIG) of American Mensa Ltd, *Modern Haiku*, *Blazevox*, *Harbinger Asylum*, *Visitant*, *Social Alternatives Journal*, *Foxtrot Uniform*, *Voice of Eve*, *Notre Dame Review*, *GUSTS*, *Porter Gulch Review*, and more.

Ꭰavid Schwartz
David is 81 years young and the author of 33 published poems and stories in recent US,UK & Canadian literary venues.

Laura Scott
I read and I write and I teach and I repeat. Oh, and I've sold books.

Jesse Sensibar
Jesse Sensibar's work has appeared in *The Tishman Review, Stoneboat Journal, Waxwing*, and others. His short fiction was shortlisted for the Bath Flash Fiction Award and the Wilda Hearne Flash Fiction Prize. He is the author of *Blood in the Asphalt: Prayers from the Highway* (Tolsun Press). You can find him at jessesensibar.com.

Ellie Sharp
ellie sharp is a college student in portland, oregon studying comparative literature. they've been published by *Blue Marble Review* and *Bitch Media*. they are also editor in chief of their college's literary magazine, *The Reed College Creative Review*.

Paul Smith
Paul Smith is a civil engineer who has worked in the construction racket for many years. He has traveled all over the place and met lots of people. Some have enriched his life. Others made him wish he or they were all dead. He likes writing poetry and fiction. He also likes Newcastle Brown Ale. If you see him, buy him one. His poetry and fiction have been published in *Convergence, Missouri Review, Literary Orphans* and other lit mags.

Sue Su
Sue Su is a Cambridge CELTA-qualified teacher with fluent English and Mandarin currently teaching Mandarin as a modern foreign language in the British School of Nanjing whilst tutoring English and Chinese privately.

Jeremy Szuder
Jeremy Szuder is a born and bred California native, raised with a tender and dedicated loyalty to the arts. His works have been published in *Fine Print Literary and Visual Arts Publication, After Happy Hour Review, All The Sins, Home Sick Zine*, several issues of *L.A. Record Magazine* as well as the 15 years

of art shows from galleries and organizations such as; Cannibal Flower, La
Luz De Jesus, Copro Nason, CoLab Gallery, and many more. Szuder lives in
Glendale California. Jeremy Szuder can be reached at jeremyszuder@gmail.
com

Jonathan van Belle

Jonathan van Belle is a copy editor for Outlier.org, an online education
platform. He previously worked as a bookseller at Powell's City of Books.
Jonathan is the author of several books, all available online, and is currently
working on his first book for Deep Overstock Publishing.

ZB Wagman

ZB Wagman is a writer based in Portland, Oregon. When not writing, he
spends his days working at the Beaverton City Library.

Patrick Wray

Patrick Wray is an artist from the North of England but now based in
London where he has worked since 2006 at the world famous bookshop
Foyles. He had recorded quite a bit music over the years and occasionally
writes articles on horror films, art and music. He publishes his first proper
graphic novel *The Flood that Did Come* in 2020 through Avery Hill. You can
see more of his art art and life at www.patrickwray.com.

Nicholas Yandell

Nicholas Yandell is a composer, who sometimes creates with words instead
of sound. In those cases, he usually ends up with fiction and occasionally
poetry. He also paints and draws, and often all these activities become
combined, because they're really not all that different from each other, and
it's all just art right?
When not working on creative projects, Nick works as a bookseller at
Powell's Books in Portland, Oregon, where he enjoys being surrounded by
a wealth of knowledge, as well as working and interacting with creatively
stimulating people. He has a website where he displays his creations; it's
nicholasyandell.com. Check it out!